Voices of Vietnam

Barry Robbins

Printed in the United States of America

Title: Voices of Vietnam

Author: Barry Robbins

Paperback ISBN: 979-8-9922852-0-8

Dedication

To Pam, my caregiver extraordinaire, without whom this work would not have been possible. Words cannot express my gratitude.

Contents

Prelude

Dear Reader,

In your hands, you hold a unique chronicle of the Vietnam War. While many books have examined this conflict, "Voices of Vietnam" takes you deeper, showing how the seeds of America's most controversial war were planted two centuries before the first U.S. combat troops landed in 1965.

To understand why Vietnam became America's most challenging conflict, we must first understand how French influence—beginning with a bishop's fateful decision to support a young prince in 1777—shaped the nation that would eventually challenge American power. The voices in these pages trace how colonialism, Catholicism, and Western influence transformed Vietnam long before Americans arrived, creating the complex society U.S. forces would find so difficult to comprehend.

The heart of this book focuses on the American war years and their aftermath (1954-1975), told through the voices of those who lived it—American soldiers and Vietnamese civilians, Saigon officials and Hanoi revolutionaries, war correspondents and village guerrillas. But these voices gain deeper meaning through the historical context provided by earlier perspectives—French missionaries and mandarins, colonial officials and resistance fighters—who show how Vietnam's response to American power was shaped by its long experience with foreign intervention.

A unique observer—Confucius himself—appears at crucial moments to reflect on how Vietnam's ancient civilization confronted and absorbed these waves of foreign influence while maintaining its essential character. His philosophical observations help us understand why Vietnam proved so resistant to outside efforts at transformation, whether French, Japanese, or American.

While these documents capture real historical events and experiences, they are not verbatim transcriptions of primary sources. Instead, they are carefully crafted representations designed to convey the authentic voices, emotions, and perspectives of those who lived through these extraordinary times. Together, they tell the story of how America became entangled in a conflict whose roots ran far deeper than most Americans understood.

May these voices help us comprehend not just the events of the Vietnam War, but why it unfolded as it did, and what it can teach us about the limits of power when confronting ancient civilizations with profound cultural resilience.

Chapter 1

The Bishop and the Prince

From the Personal Diary of Bishop Pigneau de Behaine
Apostolic Vicar of Cochinchina

Ha Tien, July 15, 1777

The young prince arrived at our mission tonight, half-starved and hunted. The Tay Son rebels had nearly caught him near Long Xuyen. Nguyen Anh—for that is his name—is barely seventeen, yet his eyes hold the weight of his family's fallen dynasty. Most of the Nguyen lords were slaughtered in Saigon. By what providence he escaped, only God knows.

My fellow missionaries urge caution. "We are men of God," Father Paul insists, "not kingmakers." But when I look at this prince, I see more than a fugitive seeking sanctuary. I see an opportunity—for our mission, for France, perhaps for Vietnam itself.

Macao, December 3, 1777

Nguyen Anh grows stronger daily. The transformation from the desperate youth who sought our protection five months ago is remarkable. He studies French with passion, eager to understand our ways. More importantly, he shows genuine interest in our faith.

Today he asked about the crucifix in my chamber. "Your God died for his people?" he said. "Such sacrifice a true king should understand." The depth of his observation startled me. This is no mere princeling seeking advantage, but a man who comprehends the burden of leadership.

The Tay Son still hunt him, but they will not find him here. More followers gather to his cause each day. I have committed our mission's resources to his protection, though I know this crosses the boundary between spiritual and temporal matters. God forgive me if I err, but I believe this prince may be the key to our future in this land.

Bangkok, March 20, 1778

Disaster upon disaster. The Siamese expedition to restore Nguyen Anh failed utterly. We barely escaped with our lives. Yet even in defeat, I saw qualities in the prince that strengthen my conviction. He rallied his remaining forces, preserved their loyalty, and protected the refugees who fled with us.

In the quiet of our temple sanctuary, he confided his fears. "Perhaps Heaven has abandoned the Nguyen cause," he said. I spoke to him of Moses wandering in the desert, of divine purposes revealed through tribulation. He listened intently, this Buddhist prince, and I saw hope kindle again in his eyes.

I have made my decision. I shall go to France myself, to plead his cause before King Louis XVI. The risks are enormous, the journey perilous, but I see no other path. Vietnam needs a strong ruler, one who will welcome both Christianity and French influence. Nguyen Anh can be that ruler, if we can secure him proper support.

Versailles, December 12, 1779

How different the palace of Versailles from our humble missions in Cochinchina! Yet as I walk these gilded halls, my thoughts remain with the exiled prince half a world away. Today I met with the King's ministers. They are intrigued by my proposals—military support in exchange for trading privileges and protection for Catholic missionaries.

Some questions cut deep. "Can this prince be trusted to honor such agreements once in power?" Perhaps not, but I kept such doubts to myself. I spoke instead of Nguyen Anh's character, his interest in Western ways, the commercial possibilities of alliance. Politics is a strange art for a missionary, yet here I am, negotiating like a diplomat.

The treaty is drawn up. France will provide ships, guns, and men. In return, Vietnam will open itself to French influence. A fair exchange, or the first step toward something more dangerous? I push such thoughts aside. We serve God's purpose, whatever may come.

Long Ho, September 10, 1789

Years of struggle, yet we make progress. French officers train Nguyen Anh's army in modern tactics. His fleet, built to European specifications, dominates the coast. The prince himself has grown into a formidable leader, blending Vietnamese tradition with Western innovations exactly as I'd hoped.

Today he spoke of his plans for reunifying Vietnam. "When I am emperor," he said, "there must be harmony between old and new, East and West." The words warmed my heart, though experience has taught me the difficulty of such balance.

I grow weary. Years of war and politics have taken their toll. Yet when I see our churches rising alongside pagodas, when I hear Vietnamese children reciting both Confucian classics and Christian prayers, I believe we are building something unique here—a bridge between worlds.

Whether that bridge will bear the weight of future ambitions, only time will tell.

Saigon, February 1, 1802

Victory at last! Nguyen Anh entered Saigon in triumph, taking the reign name Gia Long—a new dynasty born with French aid. As I watched him ascend the steps of the imperial palace, my heart swelled with pride and apprehension. Have I been God's instrument or merely a player in a greater game of empire?

Tonight he honored me as the architect of his restoration. The new emperor's generosity to our mission exceeds all hopes. Yet I see storm clouds on the horizon. Already there are those at court who whisper against foreign influence. And in France, I hear, a new empire rises under Napoleon, with appetites far greater than those of the king we first petitioned.

I am old now, and tire easily. My life's work stands completed—Vietnam united under a ruler favorable to France and tolerant of Christianity. But as I write these words, I wonder: have I built a foundation for peace or merely laid the groundwork for future conflicts? History will judge, but I will not live to see its verdict.

Let those who read these pages understand—we went forward with the best of intentions, seeking to serve both God and man. If we have instead served the cause of empire, may Heaven forgive us.

Chapter 2

A World Upended

From the Personal Diary of Nguyen Van Minh
Senior Court Official, Imperial Court of Hue

March 15, 1826

Today marks my twentieth year serving in the Emperor's court, yet never have I felt such unease. The French priests grow bolder with each passing month. This morning, I watched from my pavilion as another group of peasants gathered at their church, abandoning the rituals of their ancestors for foreign prayers.

My own nephew, Duc, has joined them. When I confronted him, he spoke of equality before their god, of salvation. "Uncle," he said, "their teachings speak to truths our own scholars have long sought." I reminded him that our Confucian teachings have served us for two thousand years. He merely smiled, the way young men do when they think age has made us blind to change.

What troubles me most is not the priests themselves—they are merely the visible signs of a deeper threat. Behind them stand French warships, French merchants, French ambitions. Last week, a trade delegation demanded new privileges in our ports. Their captain spoke with the arrogance of one who knows his cannons give weight to his words.

Emperor Minh Mang understands the danger. In yesterday's council, he spoke forcefully: "These Westerners come first with their crosses, then with their guns. Look to China if you would see our future." The opium wars our neighbors suffer show clearly what happens when Western powers gain a foothold.

June 3, 1826

The emperor has issued new edicts restricting the activities of foreign missionaries. The French consul protested immediately, his threats thinly veiled beneath diplomatic courtesy. I fear we are caught in a trap—if we allow the missionaries free rein, they undermine our traditions and authority; if we restrict them, we risk French military action.

More disturbing was the reaction in my own district. Several prominent families, now Christian converts, spoke against the edicts. They see themselves as Vietnamese but no longer fully share our values. The French priests have succeeded in creating a division within our society that may never heal.

September 12, 1826

Two French warships anchored in the bay today. From my window, I can see their guns pointed toward our citadel. The sight fills me with both rage and despair. We have stood against the Chinese, against the Mongols, against all who would rule us. But these Europeans bring weapons we cannot match and ideas that eat away at our unity.

My brother argues we should modernize, adopt Western methods and technology. "Better to learn from them than be conquered
by them," he says. Perhaps he is right, but at what cost to our
identity, our way of life?

Each morning, I burn incense at my family altar and feel the
weight of twenty generations watching me. What will they think
if ours is the generation that loses our independence? Yet what
choice do we have when their cannons can reduce our strongest
walls to rubble?

December 1, 1826

News arrived today of clashes in the south. A French priest
was arrested for preaching without permission, and in response,
their warships bombarded a coastal village. The court debates our
response, but I see in my colleagues' eyes the same fear I feel. We
are like a man facing a tiger with only a wooden sword.

The emperor has asked me to draft a response to the French
demands. I sit here late into the night, the blank paper before me
mocking my helplessness. How do I tell these foreigners we wish to
be left alone without provoking their wrath? How do we protect
our sovereignty while lacking the power to enforce our will?

My nephew Duc visited again, wearing Western clothes now.
He speaks of progress, of joining the modern world. I look at him
and see the future rushing toward us like a river in flood, washing
away everything we have known. Perhaps that is the natural order
of things—the old giving way to the new. But my heart aches for
what we are losing.

The French ships remain in the harbor, their presence a constant reminder of our vulnerability. Tomorrow I must advise the
emperor on our response to their latest demands. Tonight, I pray

to my ancestors for wisdom. But for the first time in my life, I fear even they cannot show us the path through this storm.

Chapter 3

An Evening of Questions

From the memoir of Nguyen Van Duc, written in 1845, recalling events of 1826

The three of us sat in my courtyard as evening fell—myself, my childhood friend Binh, and my cousin Tuan. The air was heavy with the scent of jasmine, and somewhere in the distance, church bells competed with temple gongs. I had invited them for this specific purpose, hoping to share the revelation that had transformed my life.

"You've changed, Duc," Binh said, studying me over his tea cup. "Your uncle says the French priests have bewitched you."

I smiled, remembering my own initial skepticism. "Not bewitched, my friend. Enlightened. Father Laurent has shown me truths that complement, not contradict, the wisdom of our ancestors."

Tuan shifted uncomfortably. "But you no longer burn incense at your family altar. Your father's spirit must be troubled."

"I honor my father's memory in new ways," I replied. "The God I now worship asks us to honor our parents, just as Confucius taught. But He offers something more—a personal relationship with the divine, not just ritual and obligation."

"Personal relationship?" Binh scoffed. "What nonsense. The gods and spirits are to be appeased, not befriended."

I leaned forward, eager to explain. "That's what I once thought. But consider this—what if the supreme force in the universe loved us as a father loves his children? What if our rituals and prayers could be more than mere transactions?"

"And your French priests taught you this?" Tuan asked, his tone skeptical but curious.

"They introduced me to these ideas, yes. But the decision to embrace them was my own. I've found answers to questions that have troubled me since childhood."

Binh's face darkened. "You speak of answers, but I see only French influence growing stronger. Their priests spread their faith while their warships fill our harbors. Coincidence?"

His words stung because they echoed my own early doubts. "I understand your suspicion. But the truth of a teaching isn't diminished by the flaws of its messengers. When Confucius's ideas spread from China, did that make them less valuable?"

"That was different," Tuan protested. "China shares our values, our way of seeing the world. These Europeans are alien to us."

"Are they?" I challenged. "They speak of compassion, of moral behavior, of serving a higher purpose. Are these ideas so foreign?"

We sat in silence for a moment, the weight of these questions hanging in the humid air. Finally, Binh spoke softly: "But what of the cost, Duc? Your uncle barely speaks to you. Some say you've betrayed your heritage."

"My heritage is part of who I am. I haven't abandoned it—I've added to it. Father Laurent says God works through all cultures, all traditions. He's helping me see how our own wisdom can be fulfilled, not replaced, by Christian teaching."

"And what of the future?" Tuan asked. "If more people convert, what becomes of our way of life?"

I looked at my two friends, seeing in their faces the same fears and doubts I had wrestled with. "Our way of life has always evolved. The Vietnam of our grandfathers was different from today's. Change comes whether we welcome it or not. Better to engage with it thoughtfully than resist blindly."

As the night deepened, our conversation continued. We spoke of heaven and earth, of tradition and change, of loyalty and truth. I didn't convince them - not then - but I saw in their questions the stirring of the same curiosity that had first led me to explore this new faith.

Years later, I would learn that Tuan had begun secretly attending Mass, while Binh remained steadfastly traditional. But that evening marked something important—a moment when three young Vietnamese men grappled honestly with the profound changes sweeping our nation, each seeking truth in his own way.

Chapter 4

Blasphemy in the Shadows

From the personal writings of Master Tran Van Dao
Royal Academy of Learning, Hue

Spring, 1826

Today I witnessed something that chills my blood. Young Duc, nephew of my honored colleague Nguyen Van Minh, walked past our academy wearing Western dress, a cross hanging from his neck. He did not even pause to bow before the Temple of Literature. This same boy who once recited the Analects with perfect clarity now spits on two thousand years of wisdom.

I immediately gathered my senior students. "Observe well," I told them, "for this is how a civilization begins to die. Not with armies or cannon fire, but with the quiet corruption of young minds."

The French priests are clever in their methods. They target the young, the ambitious, those susceptible to new ideas. Their "universal god" seems harmless enough at first—who could object to teachings of love and salvation? But beneath these honeyed words lies poison.

This evening, I wrote to the Emperor's Grand Council:

"Your Imperial Majesty and Noble Ministers,

I write with grave concerns regarding the spread of foreign religious practices among our educated youth. These are not merely spiritual matters, but threats to the very foundation of our society.

When a young man abandons his ancestral tablets for a foreign god, he does not just change his prayers. He severs the sacred bonds between past and present, living and dead. He places individual salvation above family duty. He begins to see our time-honored practices as mere superstition.

The French priests claim their teaching complements our traditions. This is like claiming a sword complements the neck it severs. Their entire worldview is built on assumptions alien to our understanding. They speak of all men being equal before their god—a concept that undermines the natural hierarchy Heaven has established. They promise personal salvation—a selfish pursuit that ignores our understanding that human beings exist as part of a greater whole.

Young Duc is not an isolated case. I hear whispers of other promising students secretly attending Mass. They're attracted by the novelty, the promise of connection to European power and knowledge. They do not see that they are exchanging their cultural birthright for a bowl of foreign porridge.

More troubling still are the signs that conversion brings divided loyalties. These Catholic converts look to Rome and Paris for guidance. They speak of universal brotherhood while forgetting their duties to family and state. How can we trust such men to serve in government positions? How can they properly perform the sacred rites that maintain harmony between Heaven and Earth?

I therefore humbly propose:

1. All students in the royal academies should be forbidden from attending Christian services

2. Converts should be barred from taking the civil service examinations

3. Stricter controls should be placed on missionary activities

4. Families should be held accountable for the religious conduct of their members

Some will call these measures harsh. But when treating a disease, kindness to the infection is cruelty to the body. We must act now, before the foreign infection spreads further through our cultural bloodstream.

With deepest respect and concern,

Tran Van Dao"

Later, as I prepared for sleep, my eldest grandson asked me why I was so troubled. I took him to our family altar, where the tablets of our ancestors stood in their proper order.

"Each of these tablets," I explained, "represents not just a person, but a link in an unbroken chain stretching back through time. Each generation preserves and passes on the accumulated wisdom of ages. Break that chain, and we become rootless, adrift in the present with no guidance from the past."

The boy nodded solemnly, but I saw in his eyes the same curiosity that has led others astray. We are losing them, one by one, to this foreign god who demands no ancestors be worshipped before him.

Tonight I burn extra incense, praying our ancestors will strengthen us against this invisible invasion that corrupts our youth and threatens our way of life. But in my heart, I fear it may already be too late.

Chapter 5

Civilizing Mission

From the Official Report and Private Letters of Admiral
François-Thomas Page
Commander, French Naval Forces in Cochinchina
December 1847

Official Report to the Minister of the Navy and Colonies:

As per your request, I provide my assessment of the deteri-
orating situation in Cochinchina. Our recent bombardment of
Tourane's harbor defenses, while successful in military terms, has
failed to produce the desired effect on Emperor Thieu Tri's policies
toward our missionaries. Indeed, these barbarians seem to inter-
pret our measured response as weakness.

The Vietnamese authorities continue their persecution of
Catholics with increasing boldness. Last month, they executed two
French missionaries in Hue, and our intelligence suggests more
are imprisoned. Our "gunboat diplomacy" clearly requires more
gunboats and less diplomacy.

The time has come to accept certain realities: The Vietnamese
court, clinging to its Chinese-derived notions of superiority, un-

derstands only force. They mistake our restraint for weakness, our civilized attempts at negotiation for fear. More importantly, they fail to grasp that France's destiny as a civilizing force in Asia cannot be denied.

From my private letters to Rear Admiral Cécille:

My dear friend,

What I cannot include in my official report, I share with you here. These three months observing the Vietnamese have convinced me that half measures will no longer suffice. While Paris debates policy, Britain extends its influence throughout Asia. We risk being left behind in the great game of empire.

You should see how they live here—in ignorance of all progress, wrapped in the moldering shroud of ancient customs. Yet when I look at this country, I see enormous potential. The harbors are excellent, the soil fertile, the population numerous enough to provide labor but not so advanced as to resist proper guidance.

Yesterday, I had an illuminating conversation with a mandarin who came to protest our blockade. The man had memorized Confucius but knew nothing of modern science or industry. When I attempted to explain why France had both the right and duty to intervene here, he responded with quotations from ancient Chinese texts! How does one reason with such people?

Personal Diary Entry - December 15, 1847:

The longer I observe this country, the more convinced I become that its submission to French authority is inevitable and necessary. Today I watched sampans crowding the river, exactly as they must have done for a thousand years. Nothing changes here unless change is forced upon them.

Our missionaries have spent decades trying to lift these people from their superstitions. They have built schools, introduced modern medicine, taught French language and culture. And how are they repaid? With persecution and martyrdom. The Vietnamese cannot say we didn't try peaceful means first.

Young Lieutenant Garnier suggested today that we might be provoking resistance by moving too aggressively. The boy has talent but lacks understanding. These Orientals respect nothing but force. The British proved this in China, and we must prove it here.

Besides, what right have they to resist? We offer civilization itself: rule of law, modern education, true religion, scientific progress. That they cling to their backwards ways only proves their need for our guidance.

Some of our missionaries worry that military action will make their work more difficult. They fail to understand that the cross and the flag must advance together. A few decades under firm French administration will accomplish more than centuries of gentle persuasion.

Private Letter to My Brother in Paris:

Henri,

You ask about my experiences here. Let me be plain: We face a critical moment. Either France will seize her destiny as a civilizing force in Asia, or we will watch as Britain and other powers divide the region among themselves.

The recent execution of missionaries provides perfect justification for stronger action. Our honor demands it, and our interests align with our honor for once. These people are like children, requiring a firm hand to guide them toward civilization. They may resist at first, but they will thank us in the end.

Some at court worry about the cost of expansion in Asia. They should rather worry about the cost of inaction. Every day we delay, our enemies grow bolder. The persecution of Christians is really a mask for their resistance to progress itself.

I tell you frankly: ten warships and two thousand men could secure all of Cochinchina for France. The investment would repay itself a hundredfold in trade, resources, and strategic advantage. More importantly, it would begin the real work of civilizing this backward nation.

What these people fail to understand is that their resistance to French influence is resistance to progress itself. They cannot be allowed to remain in their primitive state, especially not when their ports and resources could serve the cause of civilization.

Let others debate philosophy—I see things as they are. Either France will civilize Indochina, or another power will. The only real choice is whether we will fulfill our destiny or abandon it to others.

Your devoted brother,

François-Thomas

Chapter 6

The Master Observes: Harmony Disturbed

The Thoughts of Confucius Upon Viewing Annam, Year of the Metal Dragon (1848)

I, who taught of harmony between Heaven and Earth, of proper relationships and righteous governance, now walk unseen through this land of Annam. Though two thousand years have passed since I guided seekers of wisdom, my heart aches to see ancient truths threatened by strange new winds.

Here sits a Vietnamese father, his face lined with distress, as his son explains why he will no longer perform the ancestral rites. "The French priest says we must worship only one god," the young man declares. Does he not understand? When we honor our ancestors, we maintain the sacred chain that links past to present, heaven to earth. How can a society stand firm when its roots are cut?

In the royal court at Hue, I observe ministers debating how to handle the foreign presence. Some counsel resistance, others accommodation. But they ask the wrong questions. They speak of weapons and trade, when they should ask: How can moral authority be maintained when rulers must bow to foreign powers?

As I once taught, "When a prince's personal conduct is correct, his government is effective without the issuing of orders."

I pause by a village school where children once chanted the classics. Now they learn French phrases and Christian prayers. Knowledge from abroad is not inherently evil—did I not travel widely to gather wisdom? But learning must build upon tradition, not replace it. "Study the past," I taught, "if you would divine the future." These children cannot divine their future because they are losing their past.

In the marketplace, I see merchants conducting trade with Europeans. There is profit in such exchange, yet at what cost? When I spoke of righteousness in commerce, I warned that pursuit of profit must not override moral principles. These French traders bring opium along with their cloth and steel. They speak of free trade while their warships wait in the harbor. This is not righteous commerce.

A young mandarin, newly returned from a French school, tells his colleagues they must modernize or perish. There is wisdom in adaptation—did I not teach that the wise man changes with the times? But he speaks of changing not just methods but principles. He would discard the moral foundations that make civilization possible. As I taught, "The superior man understands what is right; the inferior man understands what will sell."

Most troubling are the French priests who claim their teaching complements mine. They speak of morality and virtue, yet they would break the sacred bonds between father and son, ruler and subject, the living and the dead. They promise individual salvation while ignoring collective harmony. Did I not teach that no man exists alone, that we are all threads in the great tapestry of society?

In a temple courtyard, I watch an old scholar teaching in secret, away from French oversight. He speaks my words to eager young minds: "Let the ruler be ruler, the subject be subject, the father be father, the son be son." Simple words, yet they contain the essence of social order. The French call this backwards thinking. They do not understand that when these relationships are disrupted, chaos follows as surely as night follows day.

Looking to the future, I see dark times ahead for this land. When foreign powers force change from without, the people's hearts remain unchanged. True change must come from within, guided by wisdom both old and new. As I once said, "By three methods we may learn wisdom: by reflection, which is noblest; by imitation, which is easiest; and by experience, which is bitterest." I fear the people of Annam will learn much through the bitter path.

Yet I see hope as well. In the quiet determination of those who maintain traditional virtues while facing new challenges. In the young people who seek to bridge two worlds without losing their souls. In the enduring strength of family bonds that even foreign doctrines cannot break.

Remember, people of Annam: Heaven has not changed, and the Tao remains constant. The truths I taught still light the path to harmony. Seek progress if you must, but do not forget the roots that give you strength. For as I taught long ago, "The green reed which bends in the wind is stronger than the mighty oak which breaks in a storm."

Chapter 7

Thunder from the Sea

From the Journal of Lieutenant Jules Marchand
French Naval Forces, Far East Squadron
August 31, 1858

Dawn approaches, and our squadron rides at anchor in the Bay of Tourane (Da Nang). Five warships, bristling with guns, await Admiral Rigault de Genouilly's signal. The native sampans have all fled, leaving the water empty save for our might. Through my spyglass, I observe primitive coastal defenses—earthworks that would not have impressed Vauban himself.

The men are eager. For months we've trained for this moment. France will finally teach these insolent Annamites the cost of persecuting our missionaries. The Admiral promises this will be a swift operation—one sharp lesson, and the emperor in Hue will yield to our demands.

From the recovered journal of Nguyen Van Phi,
fisherman of Tourane,
translated by his grandson in 1890

That morning, the sea was wrong. For thirty years I had read these waters like a scholar reads books, but never had they been so empty. No fishing boats, no market sampans, just five giant French ships like metal mountains on the horizon.

My eldest son, Tuan, wanted to take our boat out anyway. "The fish don't care about French or Vietnamese," he said. But my wife had dreamed of crying dragons, and in the night our ancestors had seemed restless at their altar. I kept our boat tied to its post.

Lieutenant Marchand:

0800 Hours: The signal is given. The thunder of our broadsides drowns even the officers' commands. Through the smoke, I watch our shells tear into the shoreline fortifications. The accuracy of our gunnery is magnificent. The natives respond with scattered fire—mere firecrackers against our guns.

I feel a surge of pride. This is how civilization advances, how France fulfills her destiny. These people must learn there are consequences for defying progress. A few hours of fire, and decades of resistance will crumble.

Nguyen Van Phi:

The first shells screamed like angry spirits. My granddaughter, little Mai, began to cry. We huddled in our house as the ground shook. Through cracks in the walls, I saw flames where the harbor defenses had stood. The soldiers there were sons of our village—boys I had watched grow up, who had played with my children.

The bombardment went on and on. My wife clutched our ancestors' tablets, whispering prayers. The French ships seemed like
dragons themselves now, breathing fire and death. What had we
simple people done to deserve this?

Lieutenant Marchand:

1300 Hours: Landing operations commence. The natives flee
before our advancing columns. A few try to resist—more fool they.
Our Minié rifles make short work of any opposition. These people
must learn that resistance to France is futile.

Captain Lebourg speaks of building a great port here—warehouses, docks, a railroad. I look at the primitive fishing villages and
imagine a modern city rising in its place. Surely this is better than
their backward ways.

Nguyen Van Phi:

By afternoon, foreign soldiers swarmed our streets. They kicked
down doors, shouted in their harsh language. When old Master
Thanh tried to protest, they struck him with their rifle butts. He
had taught half the village's children to read.

My son Tuan burned with shame at hiding, but what could
we do? Our spears and fishing knives meant nothing against their
weapons. Some young men talked of joining the army in Hue. My
heart ached, knowing more mothers would soon weep for their
sons.

That night, we joined the stream of refugees heading inland.
The only home I had ever known vanished behind us. My wife

wept for the ancestors' graves we were leaving behind. Little Mai asked when we could return to the sea. I had no answer.

As we walked, I heard the temple gongs sounding in the distance. They seemed to be calling out to heaven itself: "How can this be right? How can this be just?" But the gods, if they heard, gave no answer.

Lieutenant Marchand:

Evening Report: Tourane is secured. Minimal casualties on our side. Native losses unknown—they flee rather than stand and fight properly. Admiral says this is only the beginning. Soon we will have all of Cochinchina under proper administration.

I write this by lamplight in what was clearly a fisherman's hut. Simple place, but clean. Found a child's toy boat on the floor - expertly carved. Almost a shame they had to leave, but progress cannot be stopped. In a generation, their children will thank us for bringing civilization to these shores.

Nguyen Van Phi:

We spent that first night under strange trees, far from the sea's song. Around me, families who had lived as neighbors for generations huddled together, sharing what little they had carried away. An old woman sang a lullaby to her grandchild—the same song my mother once sang to me. Some things even the French could not take from us.

But as I watched the glow of fires on the horizon, where our homes still burned, I wondered: How many more nights like this lay ahead? How many more fires would we see? How many more songs would turn to silence?

The sea had been my father's life, and his father's before him, back to the time of legends. Now that life was ending. I held my sleeping granddaughter and whispered, "At least you will not remember this day, little one. But someone must remember. Someone must tell what happened when the thunder came from the sea."

Chapter 8

Emperor of a Shrinking Sky

From the Private Diary of Emperor Tu Duc
Ninth Month, Year of the Horse (1858)
Imperial Palace, Hue

How swift are Heaven's winds to change. One day I command-
ed all under sky, today these barbarians assault my realm with
impunity. The French ships at Da Nang mock our ancient sovereignty with every blast of their guns.

My ministers crowd around me like clucking hens, each with
different counsel. "Submit to their demands," urges the Minister of
Rites. "Drive them into the sea," insists the Commander of Armies.
Each speaks what he believes is wisdom, yet each reveals only how
little we truly understand these Western barbarians.

This morning I read again the reports from the coast. Our
soldiers fought bravely, but what use is courage against ships of
iron? The French guns speak a language we have not yet learned to
answer. My ancestors faced Chinese armies, Mongol fleets, Siamese
invaders—but never such weapons as these.

I am caught between Heaven and Earth. As Emperor, I cannot submit to barbarian demands without losing Heaven's mandate. Yet as father to my people, how can I send more sons to die beneath French guns? Already the refugees stream inland from Da Nang, carrying tales that shake the people's faith.

Yesterday I ordered the execution of two more Catholic priests. The French commander claims this is why they attack—to protect their missionaries. But I am no fool. These priests are merely their excuse. Did not the British use opium as their excuse to humble the great Qing Empire? These Europeans wear religion like a mask, hiding the face of conquest.

My own brother counsels modernization—to learn the barbarians' ways, to buy their weapons, to become like them to defeat them. Perhaps he is right. But I look at the great temple where my ancestors' tablets stand, and I wonder: what will remain of us once we have transformed ourselves into them?

Tonight I must write orders that will shape the destiny of our realm. My brush hovers over the paper, heavy with the weight of history. What words can turn back these iron ships? What edicts can protect our ancient ways?

The spirits of my ancestors seem to press close in the darkness. Great-grandfather Gia Long, who welcomed French aid—do you now regret the door you opened? Grandfather Minh Mang, who tried to expel the foreign priests—was your wisdom greater than we knew?

Reports say the French commander speaks of civilization and progress. Do they think us savages, we who have had writing while their ancestors painted their faces blue? We who have built ships and cities and studied the stars while they huddled in forests? Yet now their "progress" thunders from iron dragons floating on the sea.

I am forty-nine years old. In all my studies of the classics, in all the wisdom of Confucius and Mencius, I find no guidance for such times as these. How does one maintain the Mandate of Heaven when heaven itself seems to favor foreign guns?

My ministers await my decision. Submit or resist? Adapt or stand firm? Perhaps all choices lead to the same end—the slow death of everything we have been. Yet choose I must.

Tomorrow I will send my words to the French commander. I will speak of peace and negotiation, playing for time while we gather our strength. But I will not - cannot - simply yield to their demands. Let them hold Da Nang harbor. Let them think the tiger is cowed. We will watch, we will learn, and we will wait.

But in the deepest night, when even the palace guards grow drowsy at their posts, I am haunted by a terrible thought: What if these are the last days of ten thousand years of civilization? What if I am to be the emperor who lost the Mandate of Heaven to barbarian thunder?

The French shells illuminate a truth I can barely speak: the world we knew is ending. Whether by swift defeat or slow transformation, the Vietnam of our ancestors cannot survive unchanged. Perhaps my most filial duty is not to preserve the past, but to guide our people through this storm of change, even if it carries us far from familiar shores.

Heaven help us all.

Chapter 9

A Scholar's Sword

Letter from Scholar-Warrior Tran Van Khanh
Hidden Base in the Mountains of Thanh Hoa Province
Eighth Month, Year of the Rooster (1885)

Dearest Brother,

If this letter reaches you, it means our messenger has survived the French patrols. I write by lamplight in our mountain camp, where forty of us now wage war against the invaders. You would hardly recognize your scholarly brother now—my hands, once stained only with ink, are calloused from the rifle and sword.

Do not believe the French proclamations that we are merely bandits. We fight for His Majesty's righteous cause. When Emperor Ham Nghi raised the banner of Can Vuong, calling all loyal subjects to resist the French, how could I continue reciting poetry in my study while barbarians ravaged our homeland? What use is knowing the Analects if we lack the courage to act on their principles?

Our methods would shock our old teachers. We strike fast and vanish into the forests. The French call this "cowardly warfare," but as Sun Tzu taught, the wise warrior fights only on advantageous ground. When their columns march through the valleys, we attack from the hills. When they garrison a village, we strike their supply lines. Let them hold the cities—we control the countryside.

The French have their artillery and fancy rifles, but we have the people. In every village, there are eyes watching for us, mouths ready to whisper information, hands ready to feed our fighters. The French commander in Thanh Hoa has promised rewards for information about our whereabouts. He does not understand—these peasants are not merely our supporters, they are our brothers and sisters in the struggle. Their resistance takes different forms: a father who delays French messengers with wrong directions, a market woman who counts enemy patrols while selling vegetables, children who warn us of approaching soldiers.

Last week, we ambushed a French column near the Song Ma River. They were so confident in their superior weapons that they neglected basic security. We struck at dawn, killed fifteen of their soldiers, and captured their weapons before disappearing back into the mountains. By the time their reinforcements arrived, we were feasting with village supporters twenty li away.

But I must be honest—our victories come at a terrible price. The French take vengeance on any village suspected of helping us. They burn homes, seize food, and execute suspected collaborators. My heart breaks when I see the suffering our resistance brings to innocent people. Yet when I ask the villagers if we should stop, they respond with anger: "Fight on! Better to die standing than live on our knees."

Some of our fellow scholars criticize us for enrolling common peasants in our ranks. They cling to old notions of social class, even as our world changes around us. But I have learned that the son of a farmer can be as brave and clever as any mandarin's heir. In our mountain camps, scholars and peasants eat the same rice, share the same dangers, fight for the same cause. Perhaps this is the silver lining in our dark clouds—this struggle teaches us that true nobility lies in actions, not birth.

You ask about my studies—yes, even here we maintain our scholarship. Around the camp fires, I teach our fighters to read and write, while they teach me the wisdom of forest and field. We sing the old songs and compose new ones. Even our military orders contain poetic allusions that would confuse any French spy! Let the enemy think us ignorant bandits—we are the heirs of a thousand years of civilization, and we will not let them forget it.

Our spies report that the French general tells his officers this war will be over by winter. He does not understand what he faces. We are not fighting merely for territory or politics, but for our very existence as a people. Each day more men join our cause. Each French atrocity only strengthens our resolve.

I know some say we cannot win, that the French are too powerful. Perhaps they are right. But even if we fall, we will teach our children, and they will teach their children, that Vietnam has never accepted foreign domination lying down. Let the French bring their cannons and warships—we hold in our hearts something stronger than steel: the righteous spirit of resistance passed down from our ancestors.

Tomorrow we attack again. If I die, know that I fell defending the principles we learned at our father's knee. If I live, I fight on until Vietnam is free.

Your loving brother,

Khanh

P.S. Burn this letter after reading. The French are offering ten thousand francs for my head, and I would hate to make things easier for them!

Chapter 10

The Weight of Heaven

As told to French labor investigator Paul Dubois by
Nguyen Van Cu, rice farmer
Mekong Delta region, 1886
Transcribed and translated from Vietnamese

You ask about changes in our village, Monsieur? [bitter laugh]
Where should I begin? Perhaps with my father's grave, which now
lies beneath a French rubber plantation? Or with my son who died
digging their canal? The mandarin says I should not speak of such
things, but you ask, and hunger makes men bold.

Ten years ago, I worked the same land my grandfather tilled. We
were not rich, but we had enough. Each harvest, we gave portions
to the village, to the emperor's officials, to the spirits. This was the
proper order of things. Now? Now I work the same land, but as a
tenant. The French company says they own it. How can foreigners
own land that holds my ancestors' bones?

They showed papers with stamps and seals. What do I know of
such things? I cannot read French. The interpreter said we must
pay new taxes—land tax, head tax, salt tax, even tax on the palm
trees that shade my house. How does one tax the shade of a tree?

When we could not pay in coin, they took payment in land. Many families lost their fields this way. My cousin Thanh fled to the mountains rather than watch strangers take his inheritance. Sometimes I wonder if he was wiser than those of us who stayed.

The French official promises progress. He points to the new canal they are digging. "This will bring prosperity," he says. He does not mention the fever that kills the workers, or how they take men from their fields during planting season. My oldest son, Duc, was forced to work on their canal. Three months they kept him there. He came home coughing blood and died before the harvest moon. Progress, they call this?

The rice we grow now goes to their warehouses in Saigon. Our children eat cassava while Frenchmen eat our rice. Even the fish in the river are not free—there is a tax for casting nets now. My grandmother says the river spirits are angry. I think they are just sad.

Last year, they built a church in our village. The priest is a kind man who gives medicine to sick children. But he tells us our ancestors' spirits are false gods. How can my grandfather's spirit be false when his wisdom still guides us? The priest says his God offers salvation. But can his God give me back my land? Can he make my dead son breathe again?

Some young men in the village talk of resistance. They whisper about rebels in the mountains who fight the French. The mandarin warns us not to listen, but their words are like water to parched earth. What man would not dream of taking back what was stolen from him?

My wife fears I say too much. "Keep your head down," she warns. "Think of the children who still live." She is wise, my wife. But some nights, when the tax collector's seal appears in my dreams, I understand why men go to the mountains.

The French administrator talks of building a school. "Education will improve your lives," he says. Perhaps. But will it teach my remaining sons to live without land? Will it feed my daughters? The administrator has a dog that eats better meat than my family has tasted in a year.

You ask about the corvée labor, the work we must do on their roads and bridges? [shows callused hands] Count the scars, Monsieur. Each one marks a day stolen from my fields. They say we must work twelve days each year for the government. But when we count on our fingers, it is always more. Who can argue? They have guns and papers with stamps.

Last week, they posted a new tax law on the communal house. More stamps, more seals. An old woman walked up, spat in the dust, and said, "Let them tax the tears of widows, for that is all we have left to give." The clerk wrote down her name. We have not seen her since.

You write many things in your little book, Monsieur. Will your writings make my land remember it once was mine? Will your pen bring back the old ways? No? Then let me tell you one last thing. Write this carefully:

When a man has nothing left to lose, he has everything to fight for. My grandfather taught me that rice plants grow best in peaceful fields. But he also taught me that even the smallest seed can split the hardest rock, if its roots grow deep enough.

[Pause]

It grows late, Monsieur. The evening bell at the French compound is ringing. Time for me to return to land I no longer own, to plant rice I cannot keep, beneath a sky that feels heavier each year.

Perhaps that is what you truly wish to know—how it feels to become a stranger in the fields of your fathers? Ask your stamps and seals, Monsieur. Perhaps they know.

Chapter 11

The Master Views a Broken Harmony

The Thoughts of Confucius Upon Viewing Annam, Year of the Metal Tiger (1890)

I, who taught of the sacred bonds between ruler and subject, father and son, walk again through this troubled land. Forty-two years have passed since my last observation, and my heart grows heavy seeing how the Middle Kingdom's precious teachings wither in French winds.

In Saigon, I pause before what was once a Confucian temple. Now it houses a French administrative office. Inside, Vietnamese clerks in Western dress scratch at papers with foreign words. Their queues are cut, their backs bent not in scholarly contemplation but in servile obedience to new masters. When they speak to their French superiors, they use the language of equals, not the carefully graduated forms that once marked proper relationships. How can social harmony exist when the very words that define it are abandoned?

In the countryside, I see graver wounds. The traditional village, that basic unit of moral order, lies broken. French plantations sprawl across ancestral lands. The communal fields that once sustained poor families have been privatized. I watch as peasants bow now before tax collectors instead of village elders. Even the rhythm of life has changed—men forced to work on French projects cannot properly tend their ancestors' graves.

A young scholar seeks my wisdom: "Master, how can we follow the Way when the old paths are blocked? The French control the examinations now. They mock our classics as ancient superstition. To advance, we must study their language, their laws, their strange beliefs."

I tell him what I once taught: "Learning without thought is labor lost; thought without learning is perilous." But now I must add: "Yet if you would save the essence, sometimes the form must change. Study the new to preserve the old."

In a French school, I observe Vietnamese children reciting unfamiliar lessons. They learn of French heroes but not of Tran Hung Dao. They study the geography of Paris but not the sacred mountains of their homeland. Most troubling, they are taught to question everything, even filial piety itself. Did I not say that learning begins with respect for what came before?

Yet I see something unexpected. Some students take French tools and forge them into weapons of resistance. They learn of revolution and rights, then apply these ideas to their own people's suffering. Perhaps this is what I meant when I said, "By three methods we may learn wisdom: by reflection, which is noblest; by imitation, which is easiest; and by experience, which is bitterest."

In the markets, I hear women haggling in French currency over goods from French ships. The reliable patterns of commerce I once praised have given way to foreign markets beyond local control. When profit alone drives exchange, how can righteousness prevail?

Most painful is the breakdown of family order. Young men leave villages for French factories, breaking the chain of ancestral worship. Women work as servants in French households, disrupting proper domestic relations. Even in noble families, sons now mock their fathers' traditional wisdom as outdated.

Yet not all is lost. In secret places, I see scholars preserving our classics. In humble homes, parents still teach children the proper relationships. Even some who wear Western clothes bow before ancestral altars. The roots of tradition run deep, and though the old tree may be pruned by foreign hands, new shoots grow from ancient stock.

A mandarin, struggling to balance French demands with traditional duties, asks me, "Master, how can we serve two masters? The French demand we follow their ways, but our ancestors call us to different obligations."

I remind him of my teaching: "To see what is right and not to do it is want of courage." But I add: "The wise man bends like bamboo in the storm, yet keeps his roots firm in the soil. Find new ways to honor old truths."

Looking to the future, I see great upheaval ahead. These French masters think they can remake Vietnam in their image, but they do not understand. Two thousand years of civilization cannot be erased by a few decades of foreign rule. The question is not whether Vietnam will preserve its soul, but how much pain must be endured in the preservation.

I see three paths emerging: Some cling desperately to the old ways, becoming bitter and rigid. Others abandon tradition entirely, becoming empty shells of imported ideas. But a few—a precious few—seek to forge a new way, combining the moral strength of our teaching with the knowledge needed for these harsh times.

To these few, I would say: Remember that when I taught of harmony, I did not mean stagnation. When I spoke of proper relationships, I meant not blind submission but moral order. The principles remain true even when their expression must change.

As darkness falls over this troubled land, I leave this warning: A people separated from their roots will suffer, but roots too rigid to bend will break. The true Way lies in finding harmony between old and new, not in surrendering to either extreme.

May Heaven grant Vietnam the wisdom to find this path.

Chapter 12

The Price of Progress

From the Memoirs of Tran Van Minh
Chief Administrator, French Colonial Bureau of Public Works
Hanoi, 1902

Today I signed the final permits for the new railway line from
Hanoi to Haiphong. My ancestors would call me a traitor, but as
I watched the French engineers unroll their precise drawings, I felt
only pride. This railroad will bring more progress to Vietnam in
five years than we achieved in five centuries of isolation.

My son, studying medicine at the University of Paris, writes that
some of his Vietnamese classmates mock him as a "French lackey."
Easy for them to sneer from their cafes, debating revolution over
wine and pamphlets. I have seen what actual progress looks like:
clean water systems in Hanoi, modern hospitals, electric lights
pushing back the darkness. When cholera swept through last year,
it was French medicine that saved thousands.

My own journey from traditional scholar to colonial administrator raises eyebrows among both Vietnamese and French. The
old guard sees me as a turncoat; the French never quite trust me.
Neither understands that I serve neither France nor some idealized
ancient Vietnam, but the future.

I remember the moment my path became clear. It was 1887, during my examination for the mandarinate. I had spent twenty years memorizing the classics, perfecting my calligraphy, preparing to serve the emperor as my father and grandfather had done. Then a French official visited our examination hall. While we wrote elaborate essays on Confucian virtue, he spoke of railways, telegraphs, sanitation systems.

That night, I looked at my ink-stained hands and realized I was preparing for a world that no longer existed. What use were elegant essays on moral harmony when our people died of preventable diseases? What good was my perfect classical Chinese when the world now spoke the language of science and industry?

The French resident who first recruited me, Monsieur Durand, said something I've never forgotten: "There are two types of conquered peoples—those who learn from their conquerors and those who merely suffer under them." Harsh words, but true ones. Japan chose to learn. China resisted and was carved up by foreign powers. The choice seemed clear.

Some of my fellow mandarins chose retirement rather than serve the French. Others fled to join the resistance in the mountains. The most desperate committed suicide, making their deaths a final protest against the dying of their world. I chose a different path—to work with the French, to learn their secrets, to help guide Vietnam into the modern age.

This is not submission, but survival. When my son returns from Paris with his medical degree, when my daughter studies algebra in the new girls' school, when I see Vietnamese engineers working alongside French ones—this is how we truly resist. Not by clutching our past, but by mastering the knowledge that will shape our future.

Yesterday, old Master Nguyen stopped me in the street. He had been my teacher of classical literature, and the disappointment in his eyes cut deep. "You have forgotten who you are," he said. "You wear French clothes, speak their language, help them steal our country."

I wanted to tell him about the water purification system I just approved, how it will save hundreds of children in the old quarter. I wanted to show him the plans for new schools that will teach both French science and Vietnamese culture. I wanted him to understand that sometimes preservation requires change.

Instead, I merely bowed—the correct bow of student to teacher—and continued to my office. Let him think me a traitor. The ledger of history will show a different accounting.

The French themselves don't fully understand what they're creating. They see only clerks and interpreters, servants and subordinates. They don't realize that by teaching us their language, they give us access to their ideas of liberty and progress. By showing us their technology, they teach us to build our own. By training our children in their universities, they create a generation that will eventually surpass them.

My grandfather's diary sits on my desk next to French engineering manuals. In its pages, he wrote of harmony between heaven and earth, of the proper relationships that maintain the moral order. The French laugh at such ideas, seeing only superstition. They don't understand that there can be harmony in change, proper order in progress.

Each morning, before putting on my French suit and going to my French office, I burn incense at my ancestors' altar. I ask their forgiveness for straying from their path, then ask their blessing for choosing a new one. Some days, I imagine I feel their approval—not of French rule, but of learning what we must to survive it.

Let the pure ones judge me. I will continue my work. Vietnam cannot go backward to some golden age that never truly existed.

We must go forward. If that means learning from our conquerors, then let us learn everything—their strengths and their weaknesses, their science and their philosophy, their methods of creation and their tools of resistance.

The future belongs not to those who merely preserve the past, nor to those who simply imitate the foreign, but to those who can forge something new from both. This is the true meaning of progress, and its price.

Chapter 13

New Wine in Ancient Vessels

From the secret journal of Phan Chu Trinh
Written 1906-1907
Intercepted by French Security Services, 1908
Translated from Classical Chinese

It is past midnight in my study at the Dong Kinh Free School. My students have gone home, their minds burning with new ideas carried in ancient vessels. Today we analyzed the great Tang Dynasty poets—on the surface, a harmless literary exercise. But encoded in our discussion of Li Bai's imagery were messages about liberty, about nationalism, about resistance.

This is how we must work now—teaching revolution through tradition, awakening minds while appearing to preserve the old ways. The French suspect nothing. To them, we are merely old-fashioned scholars, irrelevant relics clinging to our classics. They do not understand that we are forging a new kind of weapon.

Yesterday, my colleague Phan Boi Chau sent word from Japan. His letters, hidden within shipments of tea, speak of exciting developments. The Japanese have proven that an Asian nation can modernize without losing its soul. Their students study Western science and engineering while maintaining their traditional values. Why not Vietnam?

But Boi Chau and I disagree on methods. He favors the violent path, seeking Japanese weapons and support for armed resistance. I argue that we must first transform minds before we can transform society. What use are modern weapons if we cannot build a modern nation to wield them?

In today's class, I guided my students through Mencius's teachings on the people's right to resist unjust rule. The French censor would have seen only traditional scholarship. My students saw the parallels to Rousseau and Montesquieu—European thinkers whose works I have secretly translated. When young minds grasp that our own sages taught of human rights and just governance centuries before the French Revolution, their spines straighten with pride.

Our network grows. Each week brings word of new schools opening, new printing presses running, new study groups forming. We teach young Vietnamese their true history—not the French version that portrays us as savages enlightened by colonial benevolence. We show them that Vietnam has its own diplomatic traditions, its own scientific achievements, its own philosophical depths.

But we also teach them what we must learn from the West. Through careful study of our colonizers, we learn their strengths and weaknesses. Their science, their political theories, their industrial methods—these are not Western property but human knowledge that we can and must master.

Some traditionalists call us traitors for studying Western ways. Some modernizers mock us for clinging to classical learning. Both miss the point. Vietnam needs neither blind preservation nor blind imitation, but a new synthesis. As I told my students today (dis-

cussing Du Fu's poetry while actually speaking of revolution):
"The mighty river flows ever forward, yet its waters are drawn from
ancient springs."

The French close our schools? We open new ones. They ban
our newspapers? We circulate handwritten copies. They arrest our
teachers? Others step forward. This is not the resistance of the
sword but of the brush, not of the battlefield but of the mind.

Our greatest victory came last week. A young student, the son
of a French-educated bureaucrat, came to me in tears. "Sir," he
said, "I have spent my life ashamed of being Vietnamese, thinking
we had no culture until the French came. But now I see—we
had universities when Paris was a village of mud huts. We had
poets when French was still a crude dialect. We had philosophers
questioning the nature of existence while Europeans fought with
clubs."

This is how we will win. Not by driving out the French - not yet
- but by driving out the shame and self-doubt they have planted in
our people's minds. Each young Vietnamese who stands straighter,
who sees our true heritage, who dreams of a modern Vietnam
rooted in its own soil—each one is a victory.

Tonight I work on my latest manuscript - "Ethics and the Modern Spirit." On its surface, it discusses Neo-Confucian moral philosophy. Between the lines, it outlines a path to Vietnamese modernization and independence. The French, should they intercept
it, will see only scholarly musings. My students will see a blueprint
for revolution.

They watch us, these French masters, searching for weapons
and rebel bands. They do not understand that the most dangerous
weapon is an awakened mind, that the most powerful revolutionary cell is a classroom where young Vietnamese rediscover their
heritage while learning to shape their future.

Let them watch. We will continue our work, preparing minds and hearts for the day when Vietnam rises again. Not as a replica of France, nor as a museum of the past, but as something new—a nation that draws strength from its roots while reaching for the sky.

The cock crows. Dawn approaches. I must seal this journal and prepare for another day of teaching poetry, philosophy, and revolution. The French think they are civilizing us. They do not see that we are civilizing ourselves—not according to their vision, but according to our own.

Chapter 14

Sons of Two Worlds

From the Correspondence of Nguyen Tat Thanh (later Ho Chi Minh) and his friend Pham Van Dong
Exchange of Letters, 1911-1912

(Letter from Pham Van Dong to Nguyen Tat Thanh)

Hanoi
September 15, 1911

My dear friend,

The halls of the Lycée still echo with French footsteps, but something is changing. Yesterday in philosophy class, as Monsieur Durand lectured on Rousseau's social contract, I watched our Vietnamese classmates' faces. They no longer wear the blank masks of colonial subjects dutifully absorbing foreign wisdom. They are questioning, thinking, connecting.

You were right to say that a French education is a double-edged sword. They teach us of liberty, equality, and fraternity, never imagining we might apply these principles to our own condition.

They quote Voltaire and Diderot, not realizing they are giving us weapons.

The old scholar-gentry despise us, calling us "lost children" who have abandoned Vietnamese culture for French ways. If they could see us in our private moments! Last night, several of us gathered in my room, wearing Western suits but discussing Sun Yat-sen's revolution in China. We read French radical newspapers smuggled from Paris, then debate their ideas in Vietnamese, quoting both Rousseau and Confucius.

Write soon of your experiences in Paris. We hunger for news of the wider world.

Your loyal friend,

Van Dong

(Reply from Nguyen Tat Thanh)

Paris
December 3, 1911

My dear Dong,

Paris both intoxicates and enlightens. Here, I am not a colonial subject but simply a man—albeit one who draws curious stares. I attend workers' meetings where Europeans speak of international solidarity. They talk of capitalism's victims, never realizing their own colonial system creates the very oppression they deplore.

You would be amazed at the Vietnamese community here. Sons of mandarins and wealthy merchants, sent to acquire French culture, instead acquire revolutionary consciousness. We read banned

books, attend political meetings, debate strategies for independence. Some speak of peaceful reform, others of violent revolution.
I believe both paths may be necessary.

Most telling: when we speak French here, it is not the servile
language of the colonial classroom, but the proud tongue of
Robespierre and the Communards. We are turning their language
against them, just as we will turn their education against them.

Your friend,

Tat Thanh

(Dong to Thanh)

March 20, 1912

Dear friend,

Your letters breathe fire into our spirits. Today in economics
class, Monsieur Pascal explained how colonialism brings progress
to primitive peoples. Nguyen Van Cu, whose father lost his land
to a French plantation, asked innocently whether progress might
be measured differently by those experiencing it. The class went
silent. Even Pascal seemed stunned.

More and more of our classmates speak of independence,
though still in whispers. But these are educated whispers, clothed
in Montesquieu and Marx. The French sought to create interpreters and clerks; instead, they are creating revolutionaries.

You ask about the old ways. Yes, we still burn incense at our
ancestors' altars. But beside the ancestral tablets, you might find
copies of "The Social Contract." We are becoming something new,

brother—not French, but no longer traditionally Vietnamese. Perhaps that is what our country needs.

Van Dong

(Thanh to Dong)

June 15, 1912

Dearest friend,

Your words about becoming something new strike home. Here in Paris, I see our path more clearly. We must take what is useful from France—their science, their political ideas, their industrial knowledge—while maintaining our Vietnamese soul. Education is not just learning facts but learning to think in new ways.

The French believe they are teaching us to be like them. Instead, they are teaching us to overthrow them. Every Vietnamese student who masters French law learns to see its contradictions. Everyone who studies French history learns that oppressed peoples can rise up.

Some of our compatriots here lose themselves in French culture, becoming more French than the French. Others react by rejecting everything Western. Both miss the point. We must become like the bamboo—keeping our roots deep in Vietnamese soil while growing toward new light.

The future belongs not to those who merely imitate the West, nor to those who only dream of the past, but to those who can create a new synthesis. Remember what our teacher said about revolution through education? He was right, but in ways he never imagined.

I must end here. Tonight we meet to discuss events in China. The Qing Dynasty has fallen. Old empires are not immortal after all.

Your brother in the struggle,

Tat Thanh

(Final note from French Security Service, found attached to intercepted letters)

These exchanges between lycée students bear watching. Their mastery of French culture makes them more, not less, dangerous. Recommend increased surveillance of all Western-educated Vietnamese youth. They are being transformed by French education in ways we did not intend.

Chapter 15

Seeds of Liberation

From the Personal Journal and Official Reports of Dmitri Volkov
Comintern Department of Colonial Affairs
Moscow, 1924-1925

November 15, 1924

Another long session with the Vietnamese comrade who calls himself Nguyen Ai Quoc. Unlike many of our colonial students who merely parrot revolutionary slogans, this one asks penetrating questions. Today he challenged our standard position on class struggle in colonial societies.

"In Vietnam," he said, "the revolution must be nationalist before it can be socialist. My people don't understand Marx, but they understand freedom from France."

I started to correct his ideological deviation, then stopped. Perhaps he sees something we don't. After all, Lenin himself spoke of supporting bourgeois-democratic liberation movements in the colonies. And this Nguyen has actually organized peasants, while we theorize from Moscow.

Official Report to Colonial Affairs Bureau:
RE: Indochina Situation Assessment
December 1, 1924

French Indochina presents unique opportunities for revolutionary development. Unlike British India with its complex religious divisions, or Dutch Indonesia with its island fragmentation,
Vietnam possesses:
1. Strong national identity
2. History of resistance to foreign domination
3. Educated revolutionary elite
4. Exploited peasant mass ready for mobilization
Recommend increased attention to this region. French imperial
control appears strong but shows signs of structural weakness.

Personal Journal
December 20, 1924

Long talk with Zhang from China and Nguyen from Vietnam
over vodka tonight. Fascinating contrast in approaches. Zhang
speaks of urban proletariat and Russian models. Nguyen talks
of rice farmers and village structures. I suspect Nguyen's path,
though less orthodox, may prove more effective in colonial Asia.

Something else about Nguyen—he studies us while we study
him. Behind his quiet manner and perfect Russian, I sense a mind
constantly analyzing, adapting our methods to his own purposes.
He's learning what he needs from us, not simply absorbing doctrine.

Official Assessment:
RE: Colonial Student Progress
January 15, 1925

Most promising colonial cadres this term:
- Singh (India): Strong theoretical grasp
- Zhang (China): Excellent organizational skills
- Nguyen (Vietnam): Unique synthesis of nationalist and socialist principles
Nguyen requires careful handling. His nationalist tendencies concern some comrades, but his practical understanding of peasant revolution may prove valuable. Recommend advanced training despite ideological questions.

Personal Journal
February 3, 1925

The more I work with our colonial students, the more I question some of our assumptions. We keep trying to force Asian realities into European models. Today's debate about peasant consciousness highlighted the problem.

Nguyen asked: "How can you speak of industrial proletariat in countries where 95% of people are farmers? Why should Vietnamese peasants wait for a working class that barely exists?"

Theory says colonial revolutions must follow the Russian pattern. Reality suggests otherwise. Perhaps we need new revolutionary models for Asia.

Official Report
March 20, 1925

Recent intelligence from Indochina confirms:
- Growing peasant unrest
- French investment creating small working class
- Native bourgeoisie increasingly restless
- Underground nationalist groups spreading
Recommend:
1. Increased propaganda efforts
2. Support for nationalist movements
3. Development of indigenous Communist leadership
4. Material aid to emerging resistance groups

Personal Journal
April 15, 1925

Something changed in Nguyen after today's lecture on Party structure. He was polite as always, but I sensed a new distance. Perhaps he's realized that our institutional models don't quite fit his needs.

Had a revealing conversation later. He spoke of Vietnam's villages, its ancient communal traditions. "You Russians," he said, "think you invented collective action. My people have lived it for centuries."

He's right, of course. We risk losing valuable allies by insisting they copy us exactly. The revolution may wear different faces in different lands.

Official Assessment
May 1, 1925
RE: Future Revolutionary Prospects in Colonial Asia

Most promising regions for immediate development:
1. China - urban centers ready for mobilization
2. Vietnam - strong nationalist base for revolution
3. India - massive but complicated potential
Vietnam offers unique opportunity. Small enough for controlled development, culturally unified, strategically located. Could become model for colonial liberation struggle.

Personal Journal
June 20, 1925

Nguyen leaves for Canton tomorrow. He's learned what he needed from us—organization, strategy, modern revolutionary theory. But he'll shape these tools to his own design. He's no puppet, this one.

Had a final drink together. He spoke of his vision for Vietnam—independent, modern, socially just. The socialism in his vision seems more Vietnamese than Russian, but perhaps that's as it should be.

I suspect history will hear more from him. Whether that's good or bad for our cause remains to be seen.

Final Note, December 1925

News from Canton suggests Nguyen is already adapting our methods to Asian realities. Some comrades call this ideological heresy. I call it revolutionary evolution. Reports say he has taken yet another name—now some call him Ho Chi Minh ("Bringer of Light").

Future historians take note: We think we're training colonial revolutionaries to serve our purposes. But the cleverer ones, like Nguyen, are using us to serve their own ends. Perhaps that's the real revolution—when the students surpass their teachers.

Chapter 16

Morning Flames

From the Secret Record of Village Events
Kept by Le Van Hai, Former Village Headman
Thanh Hoa Province, 1927

Three generations I have kept the village records, as my father and grandfather did before me. But now I must hide these pages beneath the floorboards, for even the act of recording our true history has become dangerous.

Today they burned the tax collector's documents in the village square. Not bandits or strangers—our own young people. My nephew Tung, who once carefully copied classical poems, led them. They sang songs I had never heard before, about revolution and justice. The French militia came too late; the ashes were already scattered to the wind.

This is not the simple banditry of the past. Something new moves through our villages. Last month, a worker returned from the Hongay coal mines. He brought papers printed in Chinese script, but the ideas were French—talk of rights, of equality, of rising up. More importantly, he brought stories of workers organizing, standing together against the overseers. Our peasants listen with different ears now.

The French increase their patrols, but they cannot stop the wind. At night, I hear voices in the bamboo grove where young men gather. They speak of events far away—strikes in Hanoi, protests in Saigon, something called a "communist party" in Canton. The world has grown larger than our village.

My son asks why I do not stop these meetings. I tell him: "When the stream changes course, the wise farmer digs new channels." In truth, I see no way to stop this current. Nor am I certain I should try.

Yesterday, Tung brought a man from Hanoi to our house. A teacher, he said, though this man's hands were too callused for classroom work. He spoke to us of the great peasant rebellions in Chinese history. But more importantly, he showed us papers—records of how much tax our district pays and how little returns to our villages. Numbers that confirmed what our empty bellies already knew.

The French administrator tells us the new taxes will fund improvements—roads, schools, hospitals. But we see only new mansions in Hanoi, new plantations where our forests once stood. Our youngest and strongest are taken for labor service, returning broken if they return at all. Even the spirits seem angry; three years of poor harvests have left the rice bins empty.

But hunger is an old companion in our village. What is new is the anger. Not the hot anger of youth—we have always had that—but something colder, more focused. The teacher from Hanoi spoke of "class consciousness," words that mean little to us. But when he spoke of organizing, of linking villages together, of standing as one—these words we understood.

Modern times bring modern weapons. Last week, the French displayed their new armored car in the district town, thinking to frighten us. But Tung and his friends merely smiled. Their weapons, they tell me, are ideas and organization. "One man with a rifle can be shot," Tung says. "A thousand men with shared purpose cannot be stopped."

I am too old to march with them, too rooted in the old ways. But I watch and record. I see how they merge new ideas with ancient customs. They talk of revolution in the morning, then burn incense to the ancestors at night. They read Marx (whoever he is) by lamplight, then consult the village fortune-teller before choosing dates for their actions.

The French think they face bandits. They do not understand that our young people now move like fish in the sea of the villages. When the militia comes, the organizers vanish like mist. But their words remain, taking root in hearts made fertile by suffering.

Tonight I heard them singing by the river—old melodies carrying new words. Songs about awakening, about throwing off chains. My granddaughter knows all the words. She is twelve.

The clever teacher who gathered tax records has gone to organize other villages. But before leaving, he told me something strange: "What you see here is happening everywhere. From the mountains to the delta, the people are awakening. Each village is a spark. Soon the sparks will become a flame."

I think of the old stories my grandmother told of the great uprisings against Chinese rule. "Vietnam," she would say, "sleeps like a water buffalo—peaceful until roused, then unstoppable."

The buffalo is waking.

More men from the mines arrived today. They speak of a network spreading through the provinces—secret messengers, hidden printing presses, channels for moving people and information. The French post their declarations. Our people post their own at night. Two worlds now exist in our village—the daylight world of submission, the shadow world of resistance.

My nephew no longer asks my permission to hold meetings. But last night he did ask for my blessing. "Uncle," he said, "we fight not just against the French, but for a new kind of village. One where the harvest is shared justly, where our children learn to read, where we stand equal with all others."

I gave my blessing, though his words frightened me. Then I watched him disappear into the darkness where his friends waited. The old fisherman's lantern by the river winked three times—their signal that the way was clear.

I am the twenty-third generation of my family to serve as keeper of village records. Our histories tell of floods and famines, of kings and conquerors, of the eternal cycle of planting and harvest. But now I record something new: the sound of our people finding their voice, the tremors of our village awakening to its own strength.

Let those who read these hidden pages in years to come understand—what began here was not simple hunger or anger. It was the birth of something that had slept in Vietnamese soil for a thousand years, waiting for the right moment to bloom.

The dawn is coming. I must hide these pages and assume my public role—the harmless old man who bows to French officials. But tonight there will be more meetings in the bamboo grove, more songs by the river, more plans drawn in the dirt and quickly erased.

The harvest of iron is approaching.

Chapter 17

The Master Sees Revolution

The Thoughts of Confucius Upon Viewing Annam, Year of the Metal Horse (1930)

I, who taught of the Proper Way, return once more to this troubled land. Forty years have passed since my last observation, and my heart trembles at what I find. The social order I praised has shattered, yet from its fragments, something new and strange takes shape.

The French masters believe they rule a pacified land. They do not see that beneath the surface of submission, revolution simmers. In a village marketplace, I watch a young woman selling newspapers. Her customers bow like peasants making simple purchases, but their eyes shine with secret purpose. The papers they buy speak of Marx and Lenin, yet they take them home and read them before ancestral altars. Heaven and revolution now share the same incense.

In a French school, I observe students reciting Voltaire and Rousseau. But in their dormitory at night, they also read the words of Mencius: "When the prince treats his subjects like grass and dirt, why should they treat him as lord and parent?" They take Western ideas of revolution and graft them onto Vietnamese roots. The tree grows strange fruit, yet it grows strong.

Most troubling—or perhaps most hopeful—is how the old forms persist even as their substance changes. Village councils still meet as they have for centuries, but now they discuss collective action rather than simple administration. The traditional respect for learning remains, but the learning itself has transformed. Young scholars quote Ho Chi Minh alongside Confucius, finding in both a path to liberation.

I pause to watch children playing in the shadow of a French factory. They sing an ancient folk song, but the words are new—speaking not of kings and seasons but of workers and freedom. When a French patrol passes, the children switch seamlessly to innocent rhymes. They have learned to live in two worlds, as their parents do.

A group of revolutionary cadres meets in a temple, their modern doctrine mixing strangely with ancient incense. Their leader speaks of class struggle, but he begins by bowing to the temple spirits. When I taught of harmony between heaven and earth, did I imagine it might look like this?

In the countryside, I find both breakdown and renewal. The traditional village structure cracks under colonial pressure, yet new forms of organization emerge. Peasants who once thought only of their own fields now speak of collective action. They use terms from European books—proletariat, bourgeoisie, dialectics—yet they understand these ideas through the lens of Vietnamese community values.

Most remarkable is how the young have taken my teachings about moral order and applied them to revolution. "If the ruler is unjust," a young radical tells his comrades, "resistance becomes the highest loyalty." He quotes me to justify overthrowing the entire system I once praised. Perhaps there is wisdom even in this misuse of wisdom.

At a secret meeting in Hanoi, I watch scholars and workers plan together—an alliance that would have been unthinkable in my day. Yet they maintain proper forms of address, proper rituals of respect. The revolution wears a Vietnamese face.

The French believe they face a simple colonial uprising. They do not understand that by teaching their language, their philosophy, their science, they have given their subjects tools of liberation. But neither do they understand how deeply Vietnamese these new ideas have become. The young revolutionaries dream not of Paris barricades but of Vietnamese independence. They speak of communism but mean national liberation.

In a villa where wealthy Vietnamese collaborate with the French, I see the other side of change. They wear French clothes, speak French words, yet they too maintain ancestral altars. Even those who seem most transformed keep some connection to tradition. The roots run deep, even in foreign soil.

What troubles me most is not the breaking of old forms—for did I not teach that the superior man adapts to changing times? What troubles me is the violence that must come. I see it in the fierce eyes of young patriots, in the desperate faces of dispossessed peasants, in the rigid posture of French officers who understand nothing of what builds around them.

Yet I also see hope. In the way young Vietnamese take foreign ideas and make them their own. In how they maintain essential values even while fighting for radical change. In their understanding that revolution must serve the people, not merely abstract ideas.

To my surprise, I find myself thinking that perhaps this revolution, foreign as its doctrines may seem, is profoundly Vietnamese. It speaks of class warfare but grows from ancient memories of resistance to foreign rule. It promises a new world but draws strength from traditional community bonds. Even its most radical leaders bow to village elders and honor ancestral spirits.

As night falls over Hanoi, I watch shadow plays on village walls. The ancient stories remain, but with new meanings. The mandarin who outwits the tiger now represents the revolutionary outwitting French authorities. The clever peasant girl who defeats the corrupt official now carries communist messages between villages. The old tales serve new purposes.

What comes will be terrible—I see the gathering storm too clearly to doubt this. But what emerges may be something unique: not a mere copy of foreign revolution, but a Vietnamese revolution. Not the destruction of tradition, but its transformation. Not the end of Vietnamese civilization, but its rebirth in new forms.

Let those who read the future understand: what grows here has roots in both Marx and Confucius, in both European enlightenment and Asian wisdom. The tree may bear strange fruit, but its roots drink from ancient waters.

I go now to make my final observation of this land. When next these people are observed, it will be by history itself.

Chapter 18

The Impossible Dance

From the Private Diary of Nguyen Van Binh
Chief Administrator, Hanoi Provincial Government
1940-1945

September 22, 1940

Tonight I burned all my French medals. Not from hatred—they were earned honestly in twenty years of civil service. But tomorrow the Japanese army enters Hanoi, and such tokens could prove fatal. Already the rumors fly: who collaborated too eagerly with the French? Who can be trusted under the new order?

The French remain in nominal control—a bizarre arrangement. We Vietnamese bureaucrats must now serve two masters, each watching us for signs of disloyalty. My French superior, Dubois, pulled me aside today. "We rely on you, Binh," he said, his eyes nervous. "Remember who your true friends are." An hour later, a Japanese colonel made a similar overture.

I think of the old proverb: "When elephants fight, the grass gets trampled." We Vietnamese are the grass.

December 15, 1940

The dance becomes more complex. This morning I attended a
French colonial administration meeting. This afternoon, a Japanese "advisory" session. Tonight, a secret gathering of Vietnamese
officials to discuss survival.

My old friend Tran, now working with the Japanese, urges me
to choose sides. "The French empire is finished," he whispers. "Asia
for the Asians!" But I've seen the brutality of Japanese rule in
China. They speak of Pan-Asian brotherhood while dreaming of
empire.

Still, I maintain correct relations with both sides. I sign French
decrees with my right hand, Japanese orders with my left, while
trying to protect our people with both.

March 3, 1941

The French puppet government and the Japanese puppet government now issue contradictory orders. Rice quotas, labor drafts,
transportation priorities—each demands precedence. We lower -
officials must somehow reconcile the impossible.

Today I approved a French rice shipment to Saigon, then quietly
warned the Japanese so they could "discover" it. They'll take the
rice, the French will blame inefficiency rather than treachery, and
our people will keep enough to survive. This is what administration has become—a deadly game of mirrors.

June 18, 1942

Something else grows in the shadows of this dual occupation. The Viet Minh—communist-led independence fighters—grow stronger. Their agents are everywhere. My own nephew has disappeared, probably to join them in the mountains.

The French search for resistance fighters by day, the Japanese by night. And we Vietnamese administrators? We write reports, attend meetings, maintain the fiction of orderly government. But everyone feels the ground shifting.

January 4, 1943

Met my Japanese liaison, Captain Tanaka, for tea. He spoke of Asian unity, but his eyes watched me like a hawk. The French administrator, Dubois, grows increasingly desperate, demanding loyalty while his empire crumbles.

I think of my father, who served the emperor before the French came. "A mandarin's first duty is to the people," he taught me. But how to serve the people when caught between predators?

The careful reports I write, the statistics I compile—all are fiction now. Both French and Japanese know this, but require the pretense of administration. Reality happens elsewhere: in midnight meetings, in whispered conversations, in careful omissions.

August 15, 1944

News of the Allied advance in Europe makes the French nervous, the Japanese aggressive. They remind me of two aging tigers, each afraid to attack the other, both taking their fear out on smaller prey.

I have begun secretly copying important documents, recording the actions of both French and Japanese officials. Perhaps history will need these records. If I survive to share them.

March 8, 1945

Disaster. The Japanese have finally moved against the French, seizing complete control. French officials who weren't arrested have fled or gone into hiding. Dubois sought refuge in my home. Despite everything, I couldn't turn him away. He's now hidden in my gardener's cottage, another secret to juggle.

The Japanese speak of Vietnamese independence under their "protection." They've installed Emperor Bao Dai as a puppet ruler. More ceremonies, more pronouncements, more lies. But now we serve only one master instead of two. Is this progress?

August 6, 1945

Rumors of a terrible new American weapon used on Japan. The Japanese officials seem distracted, frightened. The Viet Minh are moving openly now, organizing people, holding rallies. The air feels like before a monsoon, when pressure builds toward inevitable storm.

Yesterday I burned my Japanese commendations, just as I burned my French medals five years ago. Tonight I will burn this diary, keeping only the factual records of occupation stored in a safe place. Perhaps someday they will help explain how we survived this impossible time.

A final thought before these pages burn: We Vietnamese officials are often called collaborators, opportunists, servants of foreign masters. Perhaps we are. But somebody had to remain in the offices, maintain some semblance of order, try to protect our people through the art of compromise. Not everyone can fight in the mountains. Some must fight in the shadows of enemy offices.

I hear the Viet Minh are entering the city. The wheel turns again. Heaven help us all.

Chapter 19

From Tiger's Cub to Resistance Fighter

From the War Journal of Le Van Lam
Viet Minh Fighter, Cao Bang Province
1941-1945

September 15, 1941

The mountains feel different when you're hiding in them. I grew up in their shadow, knowing every trail and stream near my village. But now, training with the Viet Minh, I see them through new eyes. Each rocky outcrop is potential cover. Each bamboo grove a possible ambush site. Each hidden valley a place to train or rest or hide.

Today's lesson nearly cost me my life. Our instructor, Chi, a scarred veteran of a dozen battles, was teaching us to become invisible. "Your enemy's eyes," he said, "are drawn to movement. A man standing still is just a shadow, a rock, a tree." We practiced for hours, learning to merge with the forest.

Then came the test. A Japanese patrol—twenty soldiers with rifles and machine guns—passed within touching distance of where our group lay concealed. I could smell their leather gear, hear their breathing. One stopped so close his boot nearly touched my hand. My heart beat so loud I was certain they would hear it.

October 3, 1941

Uncle Ho arrived at our camp today. Not the fierce warrior-god some expected, but a thin man in simple clothes with gentle eyes and a wispy beard. He gathered us around the fire and asked about our families, our villages, our hopes. Then he spoke of revolution—not with fiery rhetoric, but like a teacher explaining natural laws.

"The French have ruled us for eighty years," he said. "The Japanese now claim to liberate Asia while making us slaves. But Vietnam's story is longer than either. We were fighting for independence when Paris was a village and Tokyo a fishing port."

March 15, 1942

The Tho people have taken us into their village high in the mountains. At first they were wary—too many armies have come through their lands promising friendship, bringing only trouble. But last month, when Japanese foraging parties tried to steal their rice, we helped drive the raiders away. Now they teach us their mountain ways.

Old Man Duc, their village chief, says the high places have secrets that cannot be learned quickly. "The mountain tells you where to step," he says, "but only if you learn to listen." Today he showed us how to read the mists—which ones hide you, which warn of rain, which mean Japanese patrols are moving in the valleys.

June 3, 1942

First blood today. We ambushed a Japanese supply column in the narrow pass east of Ban Thi. My hands shook so badly I could barely load my rifle. Then Chi's whistle sounded, and everything became strangely calm. The valley erupted in gunfire. Through the smoke, I saw Japanese soldiers falling. Others fired back, but at what? We were the shadows Chi taught us to be.

The captured supplies went to villages in the Red River Delta where people are starving. This is what our political officers meant about winning hearts and minds. Each bag of rice we distribute, each village we protect, builds our support among the people.

February 20, 1943

Our network spreads like morning mist through the valleys. In each village, someone watches. In each district, someone carries messages. The Japanese think they control Indochina because they hold the cities. They don't understand that real control grows from the bottom like rice from the soil.

We are building something larger than an army. In each village we secure, we help establish schools, organize health committees, set up self-defense units. The revolution grows like bamboo, each shoot helping to raise another.

March 12, 1944

The Japanese have changed. Their patrols move differently now, less like conquerors, more like hunted men. News from the coast tells of American submarines attacking their ships. The great empire that swaggered into our country now jumps at shadows—the very shadows that hide us.

Last night I led a squad of new recruits—boys from my own village—on their first mission. Watching them move through the forest, I barely recognized the clumsy farmers they were just months ago. The mountains have changed them as they changed me.

January 15, 1945

The Japanese have turned on the French. In Hanoi, they disarm their former allies, imprison French officials. Our scouts report chaos in the cities. Now both our old enemies fight each other while we grow stronger.

Out of this confusion, our real army emerges. We move openly through areas we once crept past at night. Village defense forces train in daylight. The shadow government we built through years of patient work steps into the light.

August 15, 1945

Japan surrenders. The news sweeps through our ranks like storm wind through bamboo. In our mountain camps, celebrations erupt, but our commanders keep us focused. This is the moment we trained for. As the Japanese retreat into their barracks, we advance. Each day brings reports of new towns, new districts coming under our control.

September 2, 1945

In Hanoi's Ba Dinh Square, I stood with thousands as Uncle Ho declared our independence. The words rang out clear and strong: "All men are created equal. They are endowed by their Creator with certain inalienable rights; among these are Life, Liberty, and the pursuit of Happiness."

My hands still held calluses from years of gripping a rifle. My legs ached from mountain paths. But watching our flag rise over the city, I understood what the mountains had taught us. Patience. Determination. The strength to endure. The wisdom to strike at the right moment.

Some say the real fighting lies ahead. Perhaps. But we are ready. The mountains have trained us well.

Chapter 20

When Brothers Part

Through the Eyes of Tran Van Minh

My Family's Story from the Summer of 1945
As told to my children in 1960

I was fifteen when Vietnam began to break. Not from French bullets or Japanese bombs, but from within, like a tree split by its own growing branches.

That summer of 1945, my village near Saigon buzzed with talk of independence. The Japanese were surrendering, the French were gone, and anything seemed possible. In our garden each evening, my father and his friends debated Vietnam's future while I pretended to do my homework but really listened.

My father taught mathematics at the local school, where he was known for being strict but fair. My mother ran a small shop in the market and knew everyone's business. We went to Mass every Sunday at the Catholic church, but we also kept ancestral tablets in our home like most Vietnamese families. We were modern enough to believe in independence, traditional enough to respect the old ways.

My best friend Duc lived next door. We had grown up together, swimming in the same stream, stealing mangoes from the same trees. His father was more radical than mine, hosting secret meetings where men spoke of revolution and social justice. That summer, Duc started attending those meetings. He came back full of exciting ideas about redistributing land and ending social classes.

"The Viet Minh will make Vietnam strong and free," he told me one afternoon as we fished. "Everyone will be equal. No more rich landlords exploiting poor farmers."

"But your uncle is a landlord," I said. "And he's always been good to your family."

Duc's face hardened. "Personal feelings don't matter. The old system must go."

The first real changes came gradually. Revolutionary youth groups appeared, led by people we'd never seen before. They organized meetings where they taught new patriotic songs and criticized those who had worked with the French. Some nights we heard gunshots in the distance.

Then letters began arriving from our relatives in the North. They wrote about Viet Minh cadres taking over villages, forcing people to denounce landlords and priests. My aunt wrote that their parish priest had disappeared after speaking against communism.

My father grew worried. At dinner he said, "Vietnam needs independence, yes, but not at the cost of our faith and freedom. These communists want to control not just our country but our souls."

One Sunday, a group disrupted Mass, calling our priest a "foreign agent" and demanding the church close. That afternoon, my father and other community leaders met at our house. They spoke of organizing self-defense groups. Looking through the window, I saw Duc watching from his yard. When our eyes met, he quickly turned away.

The next week, Duc's family moved to another village where the revolution was stronger. He left without saying goodbye. My mother said his father had been given a position in the new revolutionary government.

More families left, some going north to join the revolution, others moving south toward Saigon where revolutionary control was weaker. Our village split like a piece of bamboo—clean and irreparable. People who had celebrated Tet together for generations now crossed the street to avoid meeting.

One evening I found my father burning papers in the garden—photographs of himself with French colleagues, old school certificates, anything that might mark him as "reactionary" in revolutionary eyes. He saw me watching and said, "Vietnam is like a child whose parents are divorcing. Eventually, everyone must choose sides. But remember—both sides are still Vietnam."

Later that year, when the French tried to return, our village split again. Some joined the Viet Minh resistance. Others, including my family, moved to Saigon. We believed in independence but feared the communist revolution more than French colonialism. "At least with the French," my father said, "we can keep our faith and our way of life."

The last time I saw Duc was in 1954, just before the Geneva Accords divided our country. He was wearing a revolutionary uniform, passing through Saigon on his way north. We shared cigarettes near the river where we used to fish.

"You chose the wrong side," he said, but without anger.

"There shouldn't have to be sides," I answered.

We parted knowing we would be enemies. Not because of French colonialism or American intervention, but because Vietnam's own children had different dreams for their mother country. The tragedy was not that foreigners divided us, but that we divided ourselves.

Chapter 21

The Path Found

From the Private Papers of Ho Chi Minh
Written in the caves of Pac Bo, Early 1945

Tonight the spring rain drums against the cave walls. By lamplight, I sort through old papers, memories, fragments of a life spent searching. Thirty years of wandering—sailor, dishwasher, photographer, revolutionary. So many names: Nguyen Tat Thanh, Nguyen Ai Quoc, now Ho Chi Minh. Each name marking another step on the path that led me here.

I find a letter I wrote in 1919, begging the American President Wilson to support Vietnamese independence. How young I was then, how naively I believed in their fine words about self-determination! I remember standing outside Versailles in my rented suit, petition in hand, truly thinking they would listen. The great democracies spoke of freedom while treating our people like cattle. Vietnam wasn't even mentioned in the peace talks.

Here's a menu from the Carlton Hotel in London where I washed dishes. The wealthy diners never noticed the skinny Vietnamese boy studying them between loads of plates. I learned much in those kitchens—not just about Western hypocrisy, but about the dignity of common workers. The French customers who treated me like furniture were the same ones growing rich from Vietnamese rubber plantations.

Ah, this pamphlet—Lenin's "Thesis on the National and Colonial Questions." I still remember the night I first read it in Paris. My hands shook with excitement. Here, finally, was someone who understood that nationalism and social justice couldn't be separated in colonized countries. Western socialists talked about class struggle but ignored colonial peoples. Lenin saw that national liberation had to come first.

Letters from my time in Canton, teaching at the Peasant Movement Training Institute. Some of my students thought I was too focused on nationalism, not enough on pure communist doctrine. They didn't understand. I told them: "To make a revolution, you must first have people willing to die for it. Vietnamese peasants won't die for Marx and Lenin. They'll die for Vietnam."

These newspaper clippings about the 1930 Yen Bai uprising—its failure taught us hard lessons. Courage alone isn't enough. You need organization, discipline, patience. The communist structure gives us these tools. Some say I betrayed Vietnamese traditions by embracing a foreign ideology. They don't see how we've made it our own, adapted it to our culture and needs.

My old friend Phan Chu Trinh once accused me of selling my soul to Moscow. I respected him greatly, but he was wrong. I haven't sold anything—I've found a way to buy Vietnam's freedom. Communism gives us more than just an ideology. It gives us international support, military aid, a tested method of organization. Most importantly, it gives our people hope—not just for independence, but for land reform, education, modernization.

Here's a letter from a young cadre, worried that communist atheism conflicts with Vietnamese spiritual traditions. I wrote back: "Does a carpenter reject a good French saw because it's not a Vietnamese saw? We take what is useful, adapt what we must, maintain what is essential. The goal is liberation and justice. The rest is just tools."

(Later that night)

The rain has stopped. From the cave mouth, I can see stars appearing. Somewhere out there, American bombers are helping the French attack our positions. Such strange turns life takes—the nation whose democratic ideals once inspired me now supports our oppressors.

But I don't hate them. How can I? I've lived among them, seen their good and bad qualities. Their revolution against Britain helped inspire ours. Perhaps someday they'll understand that we too fight for independence, that Vietnamese communists are nationalists first. We've chosen this path not because we love Moscow, but because we love Vietnam.

The history of my journey is the journey of Vietnam—searching for a way forward that doesn't sacrifice our soul to progress or chain us to the past. I am tired now. The damp cave makes my bones ache. But the path ahead is clear at last, bought with decades of wandering, learning, struggling to find the right tools to free our people.

Let others judge my choices. History will show that we took the only road open to us. Vietnam will be independent, and our people will stand tall again. If communism helps us achieve this, then we have chosen well.

Dawn approaches. Time to put away these old papers and prepare for today's work. The past is a teacher, not a destination. Vietnam's future awaits.

Chapter 22

Sixteen Days in August

A Recollection by Nguyen Thi Mai
Former Teacher at Hang Dao School, Hanoi
Written in 1946

I was teaching grammar when the revolution came to Hanoi. Through my classroom window that August morning in 1945, I watched people gather in small groups, their whispers growing steadily louder as news of Japan's surrender spread through the streets. My students couldn't focus on their lessons—who could blame them? Even the Japanese soldiers looked lost, still carrying their rifles but with different eyes now. The mighty conquerors had become ghosts overnight.

The Viet Minh seemed to materialize from thin air. One day they were phantom whispers; the next, their flags appeared on walls, their pamphlets fluttered in the streets. Young men and women I'd known for years suddenly wore armbands, carried messages, spoke with new authority. My neighbor's son, Tuan, who I thought was just a bicycle repairman, turned out to be a local resistance leader. "Teacher Mai," he told me, "you should join the Revolutionary Committee for Education." I wondered how long he had been waiting for this moment.

The revolution unfolded like a flower. The Japanese stayed in their barracks while the French remained hidden. I watched the People's Committee take over the Mayor's office—no shots fired, they simply walked in and assumed control. The old officials melted away. My school became the "People's School" overnight. Everything changed, yet it felt both sudden and inevitable, like rain after thunder.

Strange scenes played out in Hanoi's streets. Former mandarins bowed to their servants. French-speaking bureaucrats rushed to learn Vietnamese. Everyone claimed they had always supported independence. The same police who once arrested nationalists now protected revolutionary meetings. At night, I helped write new teaching guidelines, arguing for balance while others wanted pure revolutionary doctrine. Vietnam needed independence, yes, but also wisdom.

The crowds grew larger each day. When I joined thousands marching toward the Old Quarter, we sang songs I'd never heard before yet somehow knew the words. The air crackled with excitement but also anxiety. Who really controlled Hanoi? Tuan said the Viet Minh led the revolution, but I saw other groups competing for power. Former officials tried to organize their own committees. The Japanese still held their weapons. Rumors spread about Chinese troops coming from the north, British from the south.

My students peppered me with questions about Ho Chi Minh. They'd heard he was coming to Hanoi. Some called him a mystery, others a living legend. An old man who swept my street insisted he had met Ho in 1940—the story growing more dramatic with each telling. I tried to maintain normal lessons, but how do you grade grammar exercises while history unfolds outside your window?

Then came that magnificent day in Ba Dinh Square. Surrounded by a sea of Vietnamese flags, I heard Ho Chi Minh declare our independence. He looked nothing like the superhuman figure of rumors—just a thin man in simple clothes. But his words carried immense power. When he read from the American Declaration of Independence, I felt tears on my cheeks. My father had died in a French prison dreaming of this day. If only he could have seen it.

Yet even in that moment of triumph, uncertainty lingered. We knew the French would try to return. The Chinese army approached from the north. Could our newborn independence survive? Would the revolution remember its promises of freedom and justice?

That night, watching celebration fires burn across Hanoi, I thought about my future students. I wanted them to understand how it felt when Vietnam awakened, when a people stood up, when hope and fear danced together in the summer air. We were free. We were scared. We were ready.

Chapter 23

Return to a Different Land

Lieutenant Jean-Marc Besson
3rd Colonial Infantry Regiment
Saigon, October 1945

The cheers of the French civilians in Saigon couldn't mask the silence of the Vietnamese. When our convoy rolled through the streets, past the familiar colonial buildings and manicured gardens, only European faces smiled. The natives watched from doorways and shop windows, their expressions unreadable. Even the children, who my father's prewar photos showed running alongside French vehicles, stood motionless now.

"They'll remember their place soon enough," Colonel Devier assured us at the briefing. "A few months of firm governance and everything will return to normal." He spoke of Indochina like a wayward child needing discipline. Several older officers, men who'd served here before, nodded in agreement. But something in those silent Vietnamese faces suggested otherwise.

My first hint of how much had changed came at the Continental Hotel. Before the war, my father told me, Vietnamese servants practically competed to serve French officers. Now they performed their duties with mechanical precision, eyes focused on nothing. When I attempted conversation in my schoolboy Vietnamese, the waiter responded in perfect French, his tone suggesting I was the provincial one.

My orderly, Tran, had served French officers before the war. Now he addressed me correctly but wouldn't look me in the eye. When I asked about his family, he spoke of weather and clean uniforms. One morning, I found him reading a newspaper in Vietnamese. He folded it quickly, but not before I glimpsed the headline: "Independence or Death." I pretended not to notice. The easy familiarity that old colonial hands remembered seemed permanently broken.

Last week, we swept through a village where intelligence suggested Viet Minh activity. I remembered such places from my father's photographs—peaceful hamlets where smiling peasants bowed to French authorities. But the villagers we encountered stood straight-backed, meeting our gaze. When we questioned them about resistance fighters, an old woman said simply, "This is Vietnam now." Something in her tone made our translator shift uncomfortably.

The returning colonists seem blind to these changes. At the Cercle Sportif, they discuss property reclamation and rubber prices while houseboys serve drinks with barely concealed contempt. "The Japanese occupation disrupted the natural order," Madame Devereaux declared at dinner. "But they'll remember French civilization brought them out of darkness." A Vietnamese waiter dropped a glass near her chair. Accident or message? These days, it's impossible to tell.

Henri, a captain who served here before the war, grows increasingly frustrated. "We gave them civilization, culture, order," he complained over cognac. "And this is how they repay us?" But

I find myself wondering—did we give, or did we impose? The distinction seems suddenly important. Even the architecture of Saigon feels different now—the grand colonial buildings no longer symbols of French achievement but monuments to occupation.

Today we had our first serious firefight. Not with ragged guerrillas, as our briefings predicted, but with well-organized soldiers who fought with professional skill. They struck our patrol near an old temple, their ambush perfectly planned. They fired French weapons with expert precision, struck hard, then melted away before our reinforcements arrived. Three dead, five wounded. The survivors spoke of hearing voice commands in perfect French—officers trained at our own military academies now turning their knowledge against us.

At dinner, Colonel Devier spoke confidently of crushing the rebellion. The older officers nodded, but I noticed the younger ones exchanging glances. We've seen the Viet Minh propaganda, printed on modern presses. We've heard their radio broadcasts quoting the French Revolution's own slogans about liberty and justice. In their manifestos, they write of independence with the same passion our own revolutionaries once showed. This is not the colonial uprising our commanders promised us.

Most disturbing was the incident at the marketplace. A boy, perhaps twelve, spat at our patrol. In the old days, they tell me, such disrespect would have brought swift punishment. But when our sergeant raised his hand, every Vietnamese face in the crowd turned to watch. Their expression wasn't fear—it was measurement. They were gauging us, judging our actions. The sergeant lowered his hand. In that moment, I understood: the old rules no longer applied.

Some speak of American aid, of new weapons and resources that will help us restore control. But walking these streets, watching the silent Vietnamese faces, I'm haunted by a growing certainty: we haven't returned to restore order in our colony. We've invaded a different nation, one born while we were gone. Every day brings more evidence that the Viet Minh aren't just a handful of communist agitators, as our intelligence claims, but the expression of something larger—a people's awakened sense of destiny.

In my letters home, I maintain an optimistic tone. But at night, lying awake in the humid dark, I remember that old woman's words: "This is Vietnam now." And I wonder if we're fighting not just against the Viet Minh, but against the future itself.

Chapter 24

The War Comes Back

From a recorded interview with Nguyen Van Thieu
Former Viet Minh soldier, speaking in 1960
Recalling events of late 1945 - early 1946

We thought the fighting was over. That autumn after Japan surrendered, we dared to dream of peace. In Hanoi's streets, we celebrated independence with songs and flags. Even some French residents joined our parades, talking of a new relationship between France and Vietnam. Like many young fighters, I stored my weapons and planned to return home.

But the dream lasted less than a hundred days.

I remember the exact moment I knew the war would return. A French officer addressed a crowd in Haiphong, speaking of "restoring order." But he used the same tone, the same words the Japanese had used. When someone in the crowd shouted "Vietnam Doc Lap!" - Vietnam Independent - the French troops raised their rifles. We had seen that gesture before too.

Many of my comrades were angry when the first French troops arrived, wanted to fight immediately. But Uncle Ho counseled patience. "We must show the world we tried peace first," he said. Our leaders negotiated with the French in Paris while we waited, watching the signs. More troops arriving. French administrators reclaiming their old offices. Colonial businesses demanding their property back.

Some things were different this time. We were not the same ragtag fighters who had first opposed the Japanese. Those years in the mountains had taught us organization, discipline, tactical thinking. When the French commandant demanded we surrender our weapons, we smiled politely and said yes. But for every rifle we turned in, we had three more hidden in jungle caches.

An old man in my village said something wise: "The French left as masters but returned as ghosts." They tried to recreate the colonial world that existed before Japan's conquest, but that world had died. They spoke to us as children, not realizing their own children now faced them as equals.

The first clashes came in the south. The French used troops from their African colonies, thinking Africans and Vietnamese would fight each other while the French remained clean. But we distributed leaflets in their camps, asking, "Why do slaves fight slaves while masters watch?" Some Africans deserted. Others fought half-heartedly. The French had to use their own troops after that.

In the mountains, we refreshed our old skills. The French might control the cities, but the countryside was ours. Every village had its hidden committee, every province its secret headquarters. We were better armed now—weapons taken from surrendering Japanese, bought from Chinese smugglers, even some American gear left from the war. More importantly, we had experience. Japanese attacks had taught us the art of appearing and disappearing, striking where least expected.

The French called us rebels, but we had learned to fight like a real army. Each platoon had its political officer teaching literacy between battles. We built field hospitals, training schools, ammunition workshops. In the limestone caves of Pac Bo, we even printed our own newspaper. Let the French control the radio stations—we had the people's voices.

Our greatest weapon was patience. "Strike to hurt, not to win," our commanders taught us. "Each small victory builds toward the large one." We learned to study the enemy's routines, find their weak points. French officers liked their morning coffee at exact times—sometimes those coffee breaks became very exciting.

The hardest part was watching friends die. Not just soldiers—civilians caught in French reprisals, village leaders tortured for information, families whose homes were burned for helping us. But with each French atrocity, more Vietnamese joined our cause. As my unit's political officer said, "The French are our best recruiters."

By early 1946, we knew this would be a long war. The French had tanks, planes, artillery. We had the people's support and the long memory of resistance against foreign rule. They fought for empire; we fought for our homes. My father had fought the French. His father had fought the French. Now it was my generation's turn.

But we had advantages our fathers lacked. We were better organized, better armed, better trained. Most importantly, we had seen the French defeated—first by the Germans, then by the Japanese. They were not gods or masters, just men fighting far from home for a dying cause.

Uncle Ho told us, "Nothing is more precious than independence and freedom." The French thought they were fighting scattered guerrilla bands. They didn't understand they were fighting a nation being born. Every bullet we fired, every mine we planted, every ambush we set was another birth pang of Vietnam.

Let them call us rebels. We had a better word: independence.

Chapter 25

Watching Dominoes Fall

State Department Report - For Limited Distribution
From: James W. Parker, Political Officer
U.S. Consulate, Saigon
December 1949

The ghosts of Shanghai haunt me in Saigon. Walking these steamy colonial streets, I see the same signs I saw in China before it fell: the growing communist influence, the failing French military efforts, the corrupt local government more interested in profit than survival. Even the faces of the people remind me of Shanghai—that same look of weighing options, deciding which way to jump.

Six months ago, I watched Chinese communist troops march into Shanghai while our friends there—businessmen, politicians, intellectuals who believed in democracy—begged for evacuation. Now in my nightmares, I see red flags rising over Saigon's Continental Hotel.

My superiors call me paranoid. "Vietnam isn't China," they say. "The French will handle it." But I served in China from '45 to '49.

I watched Chiang Kai-shek's government collapse despite billions in American aid. I interviewed the refugees flooding into Hong Kong. I know how quickly things can unravel.—

Today I met with Pierre Durand, an old French colonial hand. Over drinks at the Continental, he assured me everything was under control. "A few terrorists in the hills," he said, "nothing more." But his hands shook when he lit his cigarette. The same tremor I saw in Shanghai officials insisting the communist armies would never cross the Yangtze.

The French still think they're fighting a colonial rebellion. They don't see—or won't admit—that they're facing a sophisticated communist movement. Ho Chi Minh isn't some local bandit chief. He studied in Moscow, worked with the Chinese communists. His Viet Minh have turned North Vietnam into a miniature version of Mao's base areas.

Last week I interviewed refugees from the North. Their stories mirror what I heard in China: land reform, political indoctrination, elimination of "class enemies." The communists here are following the same playbook that worked so well for Mao. But when I report this, Washington responds with platitudes about supporting our French allies.

My French contacts show me maps covered with flags marking their military positions. But I remember Chiang's maps, equally impressive, equally meaningless. The French control the cities and main roads. The Viet Minh control the countryside and the people's hearts. I've seen this movie before.

The Vietnamese nationalists we might have supported years ago are mostly gone now—exiled, absorbed into the Viet Minh, or killed. Just like the Chinese middle ground disappeared between Chiang and Mao. We're letting Ho Chi Minh position himself as the only legitimate voice for Vietnamese independence, just as Mao became the only alternative to Chiang's corruption.

General Chan, my old contact in Shanghai, once told me: "You Americans think money and weapons win wars. But communists know that wars are won in people's minds." Now I watch the Viet Minh spreading their message of independence and social revolution while the French talk about restoring colonial order. Whose message speaks more strongly to Asian peoples throwing off centuries of foreign domination?

Yesterday, a Vietnamese friend—I'll call him Mr. Tam—visited my office. He fought with the French resistance in World War II, believes in democracy, hates communism. "Help us find a third way," he pleaded. "Before Vietnam must choose between French colonialism and communist revolution." I had no answer for him. In China, we waited too long to support a democratic alternative. Are we making the same mistake here?

This morning's cable from Washington asked about French military progress. They want body counts, terrain captured, strategic hamlets secured. They're asking the wrong questions. I try to explain that this is a political war, a war of ideas and loyalties. The French can win every battle and still lose Vietnam—just as Chiang won battles while China slipped through his fingers.

My warnings grow more urgent. If Vietnam falls to communism, all Southeast Asia becomes threatened. The Philippines, Thailand, Malaysia—dominoes waiting to fall. But Washington seems hypnotized by events in Europe. Asia feels distant to them. China felt distant too, until Shanghai's fall woke them too late.

Sometimes at night, I walk down to the Saigon River. The sweet rot of the tropics, the distant sound of gunfire, the political intrigues in cafes and back alleys—it all reminds me of Shanghai in '49. Different actors, same tragedy unfolding. The only question is whether America will wake up in time to prevent the same ending.

I'm not optimistic.

Addendum: Personal Note

Tonight I sat on my balcony watching the sun set over Saigon. A beautiful city, French on the surface but Asian in its bones. In the distance, I heard artillery—the French fighting phantoms in the jungle. The same sound I heard outside Shanghai as Chiang's armies fought their losing battle.

We must decide soon: either commit fully to saving Vietnam from communism or accept another red flag rising over another Asian capital. There is no middle ground left.

But we must also learn from China. Military aid alone won't win this war. We need a political vision that speaks to Asia's aspirations for independence and modernization. Otherwise, we're just replacing French colonialism with American power—and that's a losing proposition in this revolutionary age.

I only hope someone in Washington is listening this time.

Chapter 26

The Twilight of Empire

From the Command Diary of Colonel Christian de Castries
French High Command, Dien Bien Phu
May 5-7, 1954

May 5, 1954

The shelling starts precisely at dawn, as it has every day for two months. Giap's artillery, the guns we were told could never reach us, hammer our positions with metronome regularity. My operations bunker shakes with each impact. Another section of our perimeter will disappear today, another piece of French pride swallowed by the red earth of Vietnam.

Major Clement brings the morning report. We've lost thirty men overnight—not to shells or bullets, but to fever and infection. Our field hospital, itself half-collapsed, overflows with wounded. The monsoon rains have turned our trenches into sewers. Even our wine rations are exhausted. "The men need hope, Colonel," Clement says. I have none to give him.

An American observer, here to "study" our tactics, watches from the corner. His presence mocks us—the new empire coming to measure the fall of the old. "Your Vietnamese troops fought well," he tells me, missing the point entirely. They're not our Vietnamese troops anymore. They never really were.

May 6, 1954

We lose Huguette 1 before noon. Sappers tunneled under the position during the night, planted explosives. The blast threw bodies into the trees. Captain Bizot, commanding the counter-attack, reports hand-to-hand fighting in the trenches. "Like the Somme," he says, though he's too young to remember. When the smoke clears, the Viet Minh flag flies over another fallen strongpoint.

The radio crackles with Paris demanding miracles. "Hold at all costs," they say from their comfortable offices. Hold what? Every day our perimeter shrinks. The Viet Minh trenches creep closer, like fingers closing around our throat. Their propaganda broadcasts name each of our positions, each of our officers. They know us better than we know ourselves.

An artillery spotter brings photographs taken yesterday. The hills around us, which we thought were solid rock, are veined with enemy tunnels. While we waited in our fortress, they built an anthill around us. Their supply lines, which we meant to cut, run through the mountains like blood through veins. We built a wall; they built an ocean to drown it.

Tonight I walk the perimeter—what's left of it. The men snap to attention, but their eyes hold questions I cannot answer. Veterans of Normandy and North Africa, reduced to fighting for scraps of muddy ground in a valley no one had heard of six months ago. The Viet Minh broadcasts call us "the rats of Dien Bien Phu." Perhaps they're right.

May 7, 1954

The end comes faster than expected. Their final assault begins at dawn—human waves attacking from all directions. Our artillery fires its last rounds. The Foreign Legion makes its last stand. By noon, Viet Minh troops are inside our command bunker.

A young Vietnamese officer, educated in Paris, arrives to accept our surrender. The irony burns worse than defeat. He speaks perfect French, quotes Voltaire, treats us with exquisite military courtesy. As I sign the surrender document, he says softly, "The student has surpassed the master." Looking at our shattered fortress, I cannot argue.

They raise their flag over Dien Bien Phu at sunset. My men—those who still live—watch in silence. Eight thousand casualties for a valley we never should have defended. The American observer scribbles in his notebook. I want to tell him: Your turn will come. This war isn't over. It's barely begun.

In the end, we lost more than a battle here. We lost an empire, an era, an idea of French glory that sustained us for centuries. The guns are silent now. The valley returns to its ancient silence. But in the growing dark, I hear the future coming.

Vietnam is no longer ours. Perhaps it never was.

Chapter 27

Lines on Paper

From the Notes of Tran Van Dong
Member of the Democratic Republic of Vietnam Delegation
Geneva Conference, July 1954

In this elegant Swiss hotel, men in expensive suits divide my country with pencil strokes on maps. French, Chinese, British, American, Soviet—everyone has a voice except the Vietnamese. Even our own delegations, North and South, speak words written by others.

I watch Minister Pham Van Dong argue brilliantly for Vietnamese independence. But behind him stands a Chinese advisor, behind the Southern delegation stands a French one, and behind everyone loom the Americans, who refuse to sign anything but watch everything.

During breaks, I walk Geneva's clean streets, so different from bomb-cratered Hanoi. In a café, I overhear American journalists discussing the "communist threat" in Asia. They speak of Vietnam like a piece in a game. One mentions "destroying villages to save them." I want to ask him—have you ever seen a Vietnamese village? Do you know what you're saving us from?

The French delegation carries defeat in their eyes. After Dien Bien Phu, they want only a graceful exit. But they insist on "protecting" the South. The British support them. The Soviets and Chinese push us to compromise. The Americans say nothing officially but their presence fills every room.

Today they discussed the partition line. Someone proposed the 17th parallel—an arbitrary line across ancient provinces. "A temporary military demarcation," they call it. Minister Pham protests: families will be divided, economic patterns disrupted, a nation cut in half. The other delegates nod sympathetically and continue drawing lines.

In the evening, I share cognac with a French delegate I knew from university days in Paris. "You fought well," he says, "you deserve independence." Then he pauses. "But surely you understand we can't just hand the whole country to Ho Chi Minh?" I ask him if he understands that dividing Vietnam will guarantee more war. He looks away.

The Americans hold private meetings with the Southern delegation. They speak of military aid, economic support, a new anti-communist state below the 17th parallel. Our intelligence says they're already planning to replace the French as the South's protectors. One war ends, another takes shape.

A Chinese diplomat corners me at dinner. "Accept partition," he advises. "You can reunite later through elections." But his eyes say something else. China wants buffer states along its border—North Vietnam, North Korea. They've fought their own civil war. Perhaps they fear a united Vietnam would be too strong.

In the conference room, maps cover the tables. Colored lines show zones of control, proposed boundaries, population movements. The delegates debate electoral procedures, troop withdrawals, international supervisory commissions. But the real issues—independence, unity, self-determination—fade beneath technical details.

Minister Pham shows me a draft agreement. We're to withdraw forces from the South. International monitors will supervise. Elections in two years will reunify the country. But I see the holes in these promises. Who will guarantee the elections? How can there be fair voting with foreign armies present?

During another midnight session, I study the faces around the table. The French, eager to salvage something from defeat. The Americans, already planning their next moves. The Chinese and Soviets, measuring their gains. The British, thinking of their own Asian colonies. All deciding Vietnam's future.

A Southern delegate, an old friend, whispers to me during a break: "This division will tear us apart." He's right. The conference speaks of temporary partition, but we're creating permanent scars. The South will become an American project, the North a communist base. And ordinary Vietnamese will bear the cost.

Finally, the agreement takes shape. The 17th parallel becomes our Mason-Dixon line. The French will withdraw from the North, we from the South. Elections in 1956 will reunify the country. The Americans won't sign but promise not to interfere. Everyone knows these are paper promises.

At the final session, watching the delegates sign documents, I remember something my grandfather told me: "Vietnam is not a place foreigners understand. They see a small country, but we are an old nation. Our history is written in blood and survival."

Walking back to my hotel under Geneva's summer stars, I think about the line they've drawn across my country. On their maps, it looks clean and simple. They don't see the families it will break, the tragedy it will spawn. They don't understand that Vietnam's heart cannot be divided by pencil strokes.

The conference ends. The delegates return to their capitals. But in Vietnam, I fear, the real battle is just beginning.

Chapter 28
A New Strong Man

Through the Eyes of Phan Van Minh
Senior Civil Servant, Saigon
1954-1955

When Ngo Dinh Diem first arrived from exile, he seemed an answer to our prayers. A nationalist but not a communist, a Catholic but respectful of Buddhism, educated but not French-corrupted. American journalists called him "Vietnam's new strong man." We Vietnamese, tired of French failure and fearful of communist victory, desperately wanted to believe.

I remember his first speech as Prime Minister. He stood straight-backed in his white sharkskin suit, speaking of independence, modernization, true democracy. The Americans in the audience nodded approvingly. Even the French grudgingly admitted he had presence. Behind me, an old mandarin whispered, "Finally, a leader who understands both East and West."

In those early months, hope flourished. Diem moved decisively against the corrupt Binh Xuyen gangsters who had controlled Saigon's police and gambling. He stood up to the French-backed army generals. When he nationalized the police force, my French colleagues predicted chaos. Instead, for the first time in memory, Saigon's streets felt safe.

Working in the Interior Ministry, I saw the American aid pour in. New schools, hospitals, housing developments—signs of progress everywhere. The Americans seemed different from the French. They spoke of partnership, not empire. Their advisers lived in simple quarters, learned Vietnamese, ate local food. "America has no colonial ambitions," they told us. "We only want to help Vietnam stand strong against communism."

But gradually, things changed. First came the whispers about Diem's brother Nhu and his wife—their growing power, their secret deals. In my office, qualification for promotion shifted from merit to connections. Did you attend Diem's Catholic church? Did you know someone in the Nhu family? The old French nepotism in new Vietnamese form.

When Diem cancelled the promised elections to reunify North and South, he said the communists would cheat. Perhaps true. But cancelling made us look like American puppets. In the countryside, where I traveled for work, peasants asked hard questions. If Diem represented true independence, why did he fear voting? If he fought corruption, why did his family grow rich?

The Americans seemed blind to these problems. At diplomatic receptions, they praised Diem's "miracle in Southeast Asia." But their praise sounded increasingly hollow. One American adviser, after too many cocktails, confided: "We know he's a bastard, but he's our bastard."

Everything focused on fighting communism. When farmers complained about landlords, Diem's officials called them communist sympathizers. When Buddhist leaders requested religious equality, they were branded communist dupes. Diem saw red shadows everywhere, while his family treated Vietnam like a private estate.

I remember the day my illusions finally shattered. A young woman came to my office, seeking help finding her brother. He had criticized Nhu's wife at a student meeting. The secret police took him away. "But we're Catholics," she said, crying. "Our family supports the government." I could do nothing. The next week, I saw Madame Nhu at a reception, dripping with diamonds, lecturing us about sacrifice for the nation.

Now I watch Diem's "democracy" hardening into dictatorship. His Can Lao party runs everything—business, politics, military. Opposition newspapers close. Student groups disband. In the provinces, his young officials treat villagers like servants. The Americans still send aid, but their smiles look forced.

Last night at dinner, my eldest son asked why I keep working for the government. "You always taught us to be honest," he said. "How can you serve dishonesty?" I had no answer. Perhaps I'm a coward. Perhaps, like many, I fear the communists more than I hate corruption.

Or perhaps I still cling to that first hope Diem represented—a free, independent, modern Vietnam. But watching his troops close another newspaper office today, I wonder: Have we simply traded French colonialism for Vietnamese autocracy? And if this is the alternative to communism, how can we blame villagers who choose the Viet Cong?

The Americans should ask themselves these questions. But they see only what they want to see—their "miracle" in Southeast Asia, their strong man holding back the red tide. They forget that strength without justice cannot last.

I fear they will learn this lesson too late. We all will.

Chapter 29

Preventing the Next Korea

From the Private Papers of Colonel Robert S. Anderson
National Security Council Staff
1956-1957

Night after night, we rehash the same arguments in the White House basement. State Department wants more aid to Diem. Pentagon pushes for military advisers. CIA warns about communist infiltration from the North. And always, the President bringing us back to one haunting question: "Could Vietnam become another Korea?"

I've never seen General Eisenhower more troubled. As a military man, he understands what others miss—that France's defeat at Dien Bien Phu wasn't just about tactics or terrain. "The problem," he told us after one long meeting, "is that the Vietnamese people saw the French as colonizers, not liberators. We can't make the same mistake."

Yet he also believes we can't simply abandon Southeast Asia to communism. In private sessions, he sketches dominoes on his notepad—Vietnam falls, then Laos and Cambodia, then Thailand, then Malaysia. "The loss of Indochina," he says, "will cause a chain reaction we can't control."

The Korean experience weighs heavily on him. Last week, reading reports of growing Viet Cong activity, he pushed back his chair and said, "In '50, we thought Korea would be a limited action. Three years and 37,000 American dead later, we learned better. I won't send American boys into another Asian war unless I'm damn sure we can win it."

But what's the alternative? Our intelligence shows Ho Chi Minh's popularity growing. The promised elections never happened. Diem's government grows more autocratic. When I raised these concerns, Secretary Dulles interrupted: "We don't need Diem to be a democrat. We need him to be anti-communist."

The President wasn't convinced. "The problem with backing strongmen," he said, "is that they're only strong until they fall." He recalled Iran, where CIA helped overthrow Mossadegh. "Short-term victory, long-term problem."

We settled on a middle course—military advisers, economic aid, covert action against the North. "Enough to keep Vietnam from falling," as Dulles put it, "without committing ourselves to its defense." But in private, Ike questioned whether this halfway approach would work.

Last month, reviewing reports of increasing guerrilla activity, he told a story from his World War II days. "In North Africa, we had superior forces, superior equipment, superior air power. But the locals supported Rommel. Every village was his eyes and ears. You can't win that kind of war with just military power."

The Joint Chiefs want more direct involvement—air power, naval presence, maybe combat troops. But Eisenhower resists. "Once you commit ground forces," he warned them, "you're committed to victory. And victory in Asia could cost more than our nation will pay."

Yesterday, we received disturbing reports. Despite our aid, Diem's army can't control the countryside. Viet Cong recruitment grows. North Vietnam builds infiltration routes through Laos. Our military advisers request more authority, more resources.

The President studied the reports late into the night. Finally, he said something that chilled me: "We're watching a Greek tragedy unfold. We can see the end coming, but we're powerless to prevent it."

This morning, we drafted another cable authorizing more aid, more advisers. But Eisenhower added a handwritten note: "Under no circumstances should this be interpreted as a commitment to direct military intervention."

Looking at the maps on our wall—the red spots showing communist activity spreading like measles across Vietnam—I wonder if we're just postponing the inevitable. Can military advisers and economic aid really stop a popular revolution? Or are we simply setting the stage for a larger American involvement later?

The President seems to share these doubts. Today, reviewing casualty reports from terrorist attacks in Saigon, he murmured something I barely caught: "The French spent eight years learning they couldn't win this war. I pray we're not starting the same lesson."

But the cables keep going out, the aid keeps flowing, the advisers keep deploying. We're like a man at a gambling table, increasing our bets while knowing the odds are against us. Each commitment makes it harder to walk away.

Meanwhile, Vietnam bleeds. And America edges closer to decisions that will haunt us for generations.

Chapter 30

The New Order

From letters written by Professor Tran Van Binh
University of Hanoi
Intercepted by South Vietnamese Intelligence, 1958

(To his brother in Saigon - never delivered)

My dear brother,

You ask how life has changed in the North. How to explain? Imagine our childhood home completely rearranged—familiar objects in unfamiliar places, new rules about when to eat and sleep, even new words for old things.

The Party touches everything now. At the university where I teach literature, we have weekly criticism sessions. Young cadres, some barely older than my students, review our lesson plans for ideological correctness. The poems of Nguyen Du, which we once analyzed for their beauty, must now be interpreted through class struggle.

Last month, my colleague Minh made a joke about the endless meetings. The next day, students denounced him for "reactionary attitudes." He spent two weeks in re-education, came back pale and quiet. Now he volunteers for every committee, chairs every meeting, his enthusiasm almost frightening to watch.

Yet I cannot deny the energy of reconstruction. New factories rise from bomb craters. Literacy campaigns reach remote villages. Students from peasant families, who could never have attended university before, now sit in my classroom. When they speak of their parents' lives under the French, I understand why they embrace the revolution so completely.

But the cost, brother. The cost.

(To his sister in Paris - intercepted)

Dear sister,

The land reform you ask about has transformed the countryside, though not always as planned. The Party sent young cadres to classify everyone by class status. Old definitions mean nothing—a farmer with one extra water buffalo is labeled a "rich peasant exploiter."

Some classifications seem arbitrary. Our cousin Dao, who owned three rice paddies, was labeled a landlord and lost everything. His neighbor, with the same land but better Party connections, became a "progressive farmer." There is a new hierarchy now, based on revolutionary correctness rather than Confucian values.

The children are the most transformed. My ten-year-old son lectures me about capitalist exploitation. At school, they encourage children to report their parents' private conversations. Last week, little Kim from next door denounced her grandfather for keeping a picture of the last emperor. The old man disappeared for "re-education."

Yet even as I write these criticisms, I question my own reactions. Am I just another privileged intellectual, too attached to old ways? When I see young women studying engineering, peasants learning to read, free clinics in every commune—aren't these the changes Vietnam needed?

The Party says we must break eggs to make an omelet. But some days, sister, it feels like we are breaking more than eggs.

(To a former student in London - intercepted)

My young friend,

You ask about intellectual life in the New Vietnam. We have traded old constraints for new ones. Before, we worked within the boundaries of Confucian tradition. Now we work within the boundaries of revolutionary thought.

Those who adapt, survive. My department head now peppers his lectures with quotes from Marx and Lenin. "Revolutionary literature," he tells me privately, "is just the latest fashion in a centuries-old tradition of writing what authority wants to hear."

But young minds are truly changing. My students see everything through the lens of class struggle. When I taught them Kieu last semester, they dismissed its romantic elements as "feudal sentimentality" and praised only its criticism of corrupt officials.

The Party calls it "building the new socialist man." Looking at my students—disciplined, dedicated, utterly certain of their cause—I wonder what we have gained and lost in this transformation.

(Personal diary entry - found during search)

The elections promised at Geneva will never happen. The Party speaks of reunification through revolution, not votes. "The South will rise up," the cadres assure us. "The people will demand liberation."

Meanwhile, we build our half of Vietnam into something our ancestors would not recognize. Collective farms replace family plots. Cooperatives replace markets. Children teach their parents new beliefs.

Some changes I welcome. The end of child marriage. Women in professions. Modern medicine reaching remote areas. But watching neighbors inform on neighbors, children inform on parents, students inform on teachers—this feels less like liberation and more like a new kind of bondage.

Today in my classroom, discussing classical poetry, I quoted the ancient saying: "The mandarin's brush can be more powerful than the general's sword." A student immediately raised her hand: "Professor, isn't that a reactionary sentiment promoting feudal literati over the people's army?"

I gave the expected self-criticism. But later, watching the red flag fly over Hanoi's citadel, I wondered: Have we exchanged French colonialism for another kind of foreign idea? Ho Chi Minh claims to blend Marxism with Vietnamese traditions, but some days it feels like Marx is winning.

The world is changing, and we must change with it. But as I watch the old Vietnam vanish—with its beauty and its flaws, its wisdom and its injustice—I mourn what we are losing even as I hope for what we might become.

If these letters reach you, burn them. Some truths cannot be spoken in our new society.

Chapter 31

Seeds of Resistance

As told by Nguyen Van Hai to his grandson, 1980
Recalling events of 1959-60

I did not join the Viet Cong because I loved communism. I joined because Diem's men burned my rice fields.

It was 1959, and Diem's "strategic hamlet" program had come to our village near My Tho. Government troops arrived with their American advisers, telling us we had to abandon our ancestral lands and move to a new village surrounded by barbed wire. "For your protection," they said. Protection from whom? We had lived there for five generations.

When we refused to leave, they called us communist sympathizers. One morning, they burned our fields to force us out. I watched my rice blacken under the flames while a young officer from Saigon explained that this was for our own good. Behind him, an American in sunglasses took photographs.

That night, an old man came to my house. I knew him as a rice trader, nothing more. "The resistance needs good people," he said. "People who understand the land, who know the waterways." He spoke of independence, of fighting both the Saigon puppets and their American masters. But mostly he spoke of justice.

I had never cared about politics. The French were bad, but far away. Diem talked about nationalism, the communists about revolution. To me, these were just words. I cared about my fields, my family, the rhythms of planting and harvest that my father and his father had followed.

But now my fields were ashes. What choice did I have?

The first meetings were just talks—about local grievances, about Diem's corruption, about American influence. Then came military training, learning to handle weapons left from the French war. Our weapons instructor had fought at Dien Bien Phu. "Patience," he taught us. "The French seemed strong too, until they weren't."

We started small—warning villagers about government sweeps, helping people Diem's police wanted to arrest. Then came sabotage—cutting phone lines, destroying bridges the army used. Each action was explained politically. This wasn't just rebellion, they told us, but revolution. We weren't just fighters but cadres, building a new society.

I learned to move between two worlds. By day, I was still a farmer, nodding politely to government officials. By night, I attended secret meetings, carried messages, stored weapons. My wife didn't ask questions when I disappeared for days. She understood—her own brother had been arrested for refusing to relocate.

The Americans were everywhere but saw nothing. They built roads we used to transport supplies. Their aid programs gave money to corrupt officials we then taxed for our cause. They trained Diem's army in modern warfare while we learned the old ways—patience, stealth, the strength of water wearing away stone.

By 1960, we had cells in every village. Government troops controlled the roads by day, but the night belonged to us. People called us Viet Cong—Vietnamese Communists. The name meant little to me. We were farmers defending our land, neighbors protecting each other, Vietnamese refusing to be slaves again.

The political officers taught us about Marx and Lenin, about class struggle and revolution. Some believed it all. I believed in simpler things—that a man should control his own fields, that foreign armies bring only trouble, that Vietnam belonged to Vietnamese.

One night, preparing for an attack on a government post, I recognized their commander—the same officer who had burned my fields. He still had that clean uniform, that Saigon confidence. But now I had something too: conviction. Not in communism, but in resistance.

We struck at midnight. By dawn, another government post had fallen, more weapons had changed hands, more young men had joined our ranks. In Saigon, they called us bandits, terrorists. But in the villages, people sheltered us, fed us, became our eyes and ears. They understood—we were not fighting to destroy Vietnam but to reclaim it.

Years later, people ask if we knew we were making history, creating a force that would eventually humble the world's greatest power. We knew nothing so grand. We were like water buffalo against tigers—slow, patient, but impossible to defeat completely. The Americans never understood this. How could they? They thought they were fighting communism. We knew we were fighting for survival.

Now my grandson studies the war in school, learns dates and battles and political theories. But I tell him simpler truths: That revolution grows from burned fields. That resistance is born not from ideas but from anger. That Vietnam's strength lies not in weapons or ideologies, but in the stubborn determination of farmers who refuse to abandon their land.

Let others debate about communism and democracy. I know why I fought. Sometimes the smallest things—a burned field, a stolen harvest, a home destroyed—light the largest fires.

Chapter 32
The Best and Brightest

From the Personal Journal of McGeorge Bundy
National Security Advisor to President Kennedy
1961-1963

January 1961

The new administration brings such energy to Washington. Today we discussed Vietnam in the Cabinet Room—the President sharp, incisive, challenging every assumption. "If Eisenhower's approach isn't working," he said, "let's think differently."

We're all confident we can solve this. Harvard, Yale, MIT—the best minds in America focusing on one small Asian country. McNamara brings modern management techniques from Ford Motor Company. The Rostow brothers bring development theory. Taylor brings military expertise. Surely we can succeed where the French failed.

June 1961

Growing concerns about Diem. Our Ambassador reports he spends more time in church than governing. His brother Nhu and sister-in-law grow more powerful, more corrupt. But Kennedy hesitates to pressure them too hard. "Diem's the only game in town," he says.

The military wants combat troops. Kennedy refuses. "The day we deploy American infantry," he told the Joint Chiefs, "is the day we take ownership of this war." Instead, we increase advisers, expand Special Forces, send helicopters and support equipment. Limited commitment, unlimited confidence.

December 1961

Our counterinsurgency program looks impressive on paper. Strategic hamlets to protect villagers. Economic aid to win hearts and minds. Modern technology to defeat guerrilla warfare. The Pentagon briefings show steady progress—enemy casualties up, territory controlled expanding, popular support growing.

But tonight, reviewing field reports, I found disturbing details. Farmers resent being relocated. Corruption swallows aid money. The Viet Cong grow stronger despite everything we do. When I mentioned this to Bobby Kennedy, he said, "Maybe we're asking the wrong questions."

July 1962

The President grows increasingly skeptical. Today he asked about a report showing the strategic hamlet program's success.

"If we're winning," he said, "why do we need more advisers every month?"

McNamara promises better metrics, more data. But Kennedy seems to sense what none of us wants to admit—all our expertise, all our technology, all our theories about modernization and development mean little in Vietnamese villages.

December 1962

Private dinner with the President. He spoke of his World War II experience in the Pacific. "The difference," he said, "is that we knew what victory looked like then. What's victory in Vietnam? How do we get there? When do we leave?"

No one has good answers. We can't abandon Vietnam—the dominoes would fall. But we can't Americanize the war without risking another Korea. We're caught between knowing we can't win with advisers alone and fearing what full involvement would mean.

June 1963

The Buddhist crisis explodes. Monks burning themselves in Saigon's streets. Diem's sister-in-law calls it "Buddhist barbecue." Kennedy was furious. "How can we sell this war to the American people," he demanded, "when our allies act like this?"

Yet still we hesitate. Remove Diem, and who takes his place? Support him, and we own his repression. The best and brightest of American academia, and we can't solve the puzzle of Vietnam.

October 1963

Signs of coup plotting against Diem. Our Ambassador suggests we support it. Kennedy wavers—not because he wants Diem, but because he fears what comes after. "I've got too many enemies," he said today. "Castro, Khrushchev, maybe our own CIA. I don't need any more."

But events move faster than policy. Our cables to Saigon are masterpieces of ambiguity—not encouraging a coup, but not discouraging one either. Sometimes I wonder if all our intellectual prowess just makes us better at fooling ourselves.

November 1, 1963

Diem is gone—murdered after the coup we didn't support but didn't prevent. Kennedy seems shaken. "This is why I hate the CIA business," he told me. "Once you start down that road..."

We tell ourselves Vietnam will be easier now. New leadership, new start. But looking at the cables from Saigon—confusion in the streets, communists taking advantage, soldiers uncertain who to obey—I wonder if we've opened Pandora's box.

November 22, 1963

The President is dead. In our last discussion about Vietnam, two days ago, he talked about re-evaluating our entire approach after the '64 election. "No one's figured out how to beat a political insurgency with military power," he said. "Maybe it's time to cut our losses."

Now Johnson takes over, promising to continue Kennedy's policies. But which policies? The public commitment to stand firm? Or the private doubts about whether Vietnam was worth the cost?

Tonight, reviewing our Vietnam files, I'm struck by how our confidence has eroded. We came in certain that American knowledge, technology, and determination could solve any problem. We're ending the year wondering if some problems have no American solution.

The tragedy isn't just that we were wrong. It's that we were wrong with the best of intentions, the finest minds, the noblest goals. If the best and brightest couldn't solve Vietnam, what does that say about America's ability to shape the world?

Chapter 33

The Last Meditation

Final Thoughts of Thich Tam Tung
Before Self-Immolation
Saigon, August 1963

The gasoline soaks my robe, cold against my skin. Strange—after thirty years of meditation, to still notice physical sensations at such a moment. The American photographer has taken his position. Good. The world must witness.

Traffic continues on the street before me. A woman hurries past with her market basket. Students laugh at a sidewalk café. Soon they will remember this ordinary moment forever. I pray they understand—this is not a death, but a message. What words cannot say, perhaps flames can.

This morning I performed the ritual sweeping of the temple courtyard one last time. For years we worked within the system—respectful petitions, humble requests for religious equality. Diem's people called it political agitation. The police closed our temples, arrested our monks, forbade our ceremonies. They thought they could suppress the dharma with guns and prisons.

The matchbox rests in my palm. Inside, three matches. In case the first two fail—even now, I think practically. My disciples wanted to douse themselves instead. "I am old," I told them. "I have lived my life." They must stay to continue the struggle. Already Diem's sister-in-law mocks us as "barbecuing bonzes." Let her mock. The world will remember.

A breeze stirs the hem of my robe. I remember my first day as a novice, how strange the saffron cloth felt. Now it will become my funeral pyre. The Buddha taught that all is impermanent, all is suffering, all is without self. Even this gasoline-soaked body is merely borrowed matter, soon to be returned to the elements.

Yesterday, police shot two children for carrying Buddhist flags. Their mother came to the temple, not crying, just silent. How many such silent sufferers walk Saigon's streets? Our president, who claims to serve democracy, dines with his Catholic bishops while Buddhist parents bury their children. His American allies speak of freedom while funding the forces that oppress us.

The sun reaches the position we chose. The shadows will not interfere with the photographers. Amazing, these technical considerations for an act of supreme sacrifice. But it must be witnessed, must be recorded. In our connected world, flames in Saigon will illuminate darkness in Washington.

I hear the police whistle—they have spotted our gathering. No matter. They cannot reach me in time. These last moments belong to me alone. I have written no letter, made no declaration. The flames will speak.

My legs hold the lotus position without effort, thirty years of muscle memory. The metal of the matchbox grows warm in my hand. Time telescopes—I am a child learning the sutras, a young monk sweeping temple steps, an old man watching my country tear itself apart.

I do not hate Diem or his family. Hate is a chain that binds both hater and hated. I seek only to shine light on truth. Buddhism has survived emperors and kings, warlords and colonizers. It will survive Diem. But how many more will suffer before these wounds heal?

The police are running now, pushing through the crowd. The photographer raises his camera. A woman begins to cry. All is prepared. All is ready.

To those who will call this suicide, I say: look deeper. When a man burns himself to warm others, is this death? When the rain gives itself to the dry earth, is this destruction? We are not separate, this body and the air it will become, these flames and the light they cast, this moment and the change it will birth.

I feel only peace now. The gasoline no longer feels cold. The noises of the street fade. There is only the matchbox, the sun, and the inevitable next moment.

May all beings be free from suffering.

The match flares bright -

Chapter 34

Something in the Dark

From the Combat Log of Lieutenant James Morrison
USS Maddox (DD-731)
August 2-4, 1964
Gulf of Tonkin

August 2, 1964

The first engagement was real enough. Three North Vietnamese torpedo boats attacked us in broad daylight. No ambiguity there—we could see them, count them, watch their wakes as they charged. We fired, they fired, they retreated. Clean, clear combat.

But this evening...something's wrong with what they're telling Washington.

I was on the bridge. Yes, we were fired on. Yes, we returned fire. But the damage report claimed our ship was hit. I saw no damage. The after-action report mentioned multiple torpedo boats. I saw unclear radar contacts in rough seas.

Captain Herrick seems troubled. I overheard him telling the XO, "They want certainty. I can only give them what we saw—and what we saw isn't what they're reporting."

August 4, 1964

Tonight everything became mud. Radar contacts appearing and disappearing. Sonar reporting torpedoes that nobody saw. Gunners firing at shapes in the darkness. The USS Turner Joy reporting the same chaos—shadows, maybes, might-have-beens.

At 2047, Captain Herrick sent a cable: "Review of action makes many reported contacts and torpedoes fired appear doubtful...S uggest complete evaluation before any further action taken."

But by then, Washington had already decided. President Johnson was on television announcing retaliation while we were still trying to figure out what, if anything, had actually happened.

The raid orders came in before midnight. Our aircraft were bombing North Vietnam while we were still writing up conflicting reports about what we'd encountered.

Later that night, I found Chief Reynolds, our most experienced sonar operator, staring into his coffee in the wardroom.

"What really happened out there, Chief?"

He looked at me for a long moment. "Sir, in weather like that, with the sea conditions we had...sonar shows all kinds of ghosts. Weather effects. Biological effects. Our own ship's noise bouncing back at us."

"But Washington's saying it was a clear attack."

"Washington wasn't out here in the dark with us, sir."

August 5, 1964

The headlines are calling it an "unprovoked attack." Politicians demand retaliation. But our own combat logs tell a different story—or rather, no clear story at all.

What we know: We were operating close to North Vietnam's coast, supporting South Vietnamese raids. We detected radar contacts. Our nerves were on edge after the August 2nd incident. The sea was rough, the night dark.

What we don't know: Whether those radar contacts were real boats. Whether the torpedoes our sonar detected were real or false echoes. Whether we were shooting at enemies or shadows.

Yet now we're at war. Congress is passing the Gulf of Tonkin Resolution. Our response to something that may not have happened will give the President power to escalate the war without further Congressional approval.

I studied navigation at Annapolis—the science of knowing exactly where you are. But tonight, writing this log, I feel lost. When does an assumption become a fact? When does a possibility become an excuse? When does a shadow in the dark become a reason for war?

The Captain just radioed our final report: "Whole event appears very doubtful." But like radio signals in a storm, the truth is already lost in the static of politics and headlines.

Years from now, someone will ask me if North Vietnam really attacked us that night in the Gulf of Tonkin. I'll have to answer honestly: I was there, and I'm still not sure.

But I am sure of what came after. The bombers. The resolution. The escalation. A war built on shadows in the dark.

God help us all.

Chapter 35

Welcome to the Nam

From letters of PFC Michael Doyle
First Battalion, Ninth Marines
Da Nang, March 1965

Dear Mom,

Remember those World War II movies Dad loved, with Marines storming beaches? Well, we didn't storm anything. We waded through a crowd of Vietnamese girls throwing flower petals. Some welcome committee—they even had a brass band playing "The Stars and Stripes Forever" slightly off-key.

The official line is we're here to protect the air base. Defensive positions only. But if that's true, why did we bring so much o-ffensive weaponry? And why are they building permanent barracks instead of temporary ones?

Colonel gives daily speeches about "protecting democracy" and "containing communism." Most of us just nod and sweat. It's so hot here, Mom. The air feels like hot soup.

More later—they're calling us for perimeter duty.

Love, Mike

Dear Dad,

You asked what it's like here. Remember telling me about arriving in France in '44? How the French treated you like liberators? It's different here. The Vietnamese smile and bow, but their eyes follow us everywhere. Even the kids who beg for candy watch us like hawks.

We patrol the hills around the airfield. Beautiful country—green mountains rolling down to the South China Sea. Hard to believe there's a war on. Then you notice the helicopter gunships coming and going, the constant thunder of jets taking off.

Yesterday, a Vietnamese worker on the base asked me, "How long you stay in Vietnam?" Before I could answer, my sergeant said, "Until we win, buddy. Until we win."

The Vietnamese guy just smiled that smile they all have—like they know something we don't.

Your son, Mike

Dear Sarah [sister],

You asked about the Vietnamese people. Hard to figure them out. The ones who work on base are friendly enough. But in the villages, they shut their doors when we patrol through. Can't tell who's friendly and who isn't.

Our interpreter, who we call Charlie (yeah, I know—same as what we call the enemy), tries to explain their culture to us. All about saving face, respecting elders, ancestor worship. But he also says most villagers just want to be left alone to plant their rice and raise their kids.

"Why don't they choose sides then?" I asked him. "Help us fight the Viet Cong?"

He gave me that Vietnamese smile and said, "Choose sides? The buffalo does not choose between tigers fighting in the jungle."

I'm still trying to figure out what he meant.

Love, Mike

Dear Mom,

Don't worry about what you see on TV. We're still mostly doing guard duty. But things are changing. More troops arrive every day. They're building big supply dumps, ammunition stores, fuel tanks. Looks less like a defensive operation and more like preparation for a major campaign.

The old-timers (guys who've been here three whole months) say the Viet Cong are out there in the hills, watching. Sometimes at night, we see signals flashing on the mountainsides. The South Vietnamese troops say it's just farmers with lanterns. But the signals seem awful organized for farmers.

Last night, a mortar round hit the runway. Just one. Like they're reminding us they're still here.

Love, Mike

Dear Dad,

Remember how you said the scariest part of war was the waiting? Now I understand. We spend hours in the sun, watching tree lines that never move. Then one shot rings out, everyone hits the dirt, and...nothing. Just silence and more waiting.

The brass says we're winning hearts and minds. We hand out candy to kids, medicine to villages. But last week, three Marines stepped on mines in a "friendly" village. The villagers said they didn't know anything about it. Just smiled those smiles.

Colonel says we're writing history—first American combat troops in Vietnam. Somehow I don't think it'll be that simple. Even the South Vietnamese army guys look at us like we don't understand what we're getting into.

Got to go—my turn for watch.

Your son, Mike

[Personal diary entry]

Things I can't write home about:

The fear. Not of fighting—we haven't really fought yet. But this feeling of being watched. Like the whole country is one big ambush waiting to happen.

The doubt. We're supposed to be defending South Vietnam from communist aggression. But which Vietnamese are we defending? The generals in Saigon with their French wines and American cars? The villagers who close their doors when we pass? The workers on base who might be counting our supplies for the Viet Cong?

The growing certainty that this is just the beginning. They're building too much, bringing in too many men, for this to be just base defense. Whatever they're planning, I don't think we'll be going home soon.

Charlie, our interpreter, told me an old Vietnamese proverb today: "The elephant and the tiger may battle, but the grass suffers most." I'm starting to think we're the elephant in that story.

And I'm starting to wonder if the grass knows something we don't.

Chapter 36

The New Masters

From the diary of Tran Thi Mai
Schoolteacher, Da Nang
March-April 1965

The Americans arrived like a circus coming to town. City officials ordered us to line the streets, throw flower petals, smile and wave. "Show gratitude to our protectors," they said. My third-grade students practiced "The Star-Spangled Banner" for two weeks. The irony was not lost on my older colleagues—we performed similar welcomes for the Japanese, then the returning French. Vietnam has long experience welcoming foreign saviors.

Behind the smiles, we whisper: Are they different from the French? Already they build their separate world—PX stores we cannot enter, clubs where only they can drink, new brothels opening every week. Their money changes everything. A week's teacher salary buys one American cigarette pack on the black market. Rice prices soar because farmers can make more money doing laundry for GIs than working their fields.

My classroom windows face their airbase. Each day more planes, more helicopters, more noise. My students no longer jump when bombs shake the building. They just pause in their recitation, wait for the noise to pass, then continue. Children should not be so familiar with the sounds of war. Last week, little Kim drew a picture of her house. She included helicopter gunships in the sky as naturally as she drew the sun and clouds.

The Americans mean well, I suppose. They build schools and clinics, hand out food and medicine. But there is something insulting in their generosity—as if we were all children needing their care. When they visit our school, they pat students' heads like puppies. They seem unable to understand that Vietnam had universities when their ancestors were burning witches.

My neighbor's daughter works as a translator on the base. She says the Americans have endless meetings about "winning hearts and minds." Yet they cannot see how their very presence creates resentment. Every bar girl walking with a GI, every farmer's field bulldozed for their projects, every village relocated for "strategic purposes" pushes more people toward the Viet Cong.

Yesterday, American soldiers gave candy to my students. The children bowed politely, said "thank you" in careful English. Later, I found the candy in the waste basket. "Teacher," they explained, "our parents say don't eat their food. Don't trust them like we trusted the French." Even children understand—kindness from foreign armies comes with a price.

The changes come so quickly now. Last year, Da Nang was a quiet provincial city. Now it bustles with soldiers, prostitutes, black marketers. Peasants abandon their farms to work as laborers. Students drop out to sell cigarettes to GIs. The Americans call this progress. I call it the destruction of our society.

My father, who survived both French and Japanese occupations, says it best: "The Americans will destroy Vietnam in order to save it. At least the French only wanted our labor. The Americans want our souls."

At night, lying in bed, I hear their helicopters circling the city. In my courtyard, the frangipani tree my grandfather planted still blooms, its sweet scent mixing with diesel fumes from passing American trucks. Like the tree, Vietnam endures. But for how long? How many more armies must we welcome with flowers while holding fear in our hearts?

Today a student asked me, "Teacher, when will Vietnam belong to Vietnamese?" I had no answer. Looking at the American bases growing like mushrooms after rain, the jets screaming overhead, the endless convoys of trucks and tanks, I wonder if anyone remembers what Vietnam was like before foreign armies came to "save" us.

How many more generations of Vietnamese children will grow up thinking war is normal, thinking foreign soldiers in their streets is natural, thinking their country belongs to others?

Chapter 37

Counting Their Steps

Report from Comrade Nguyen
Political Officer, Viet Cong B-4 Cell
Da Nang Area Command
April 1965

The Americans build as if they plan to stay forever. Each day more materials arrive—cement, steel, entire buildings in pieces. Our workers on the base count every truck, note every supply dump. Their preparations tell us much about their intentions. Already their base at Da Nang is larger than anything the French built in twenty years of occupation.

They are confident, these new soldiers. They walk in groups, laughing loudly, pointing at ancient temples like tourists. They do not check rooftops. They do not notice who watches them. When they patrol, they talk and smoke. In the villages, they give candy to children, never wondering which fathers are our fighters. Even their officers move with the arrogance of those who believe technology conquers all.

Their equipment impresses—helicopters that hunt like hawks, jets that shake the earth, weapons we've never seen. Each soldier carries more firepower than an entire Viet Minh squad in the

French war. But we see weaknesses too. They depend on machines, on supplies, on long lines of transport. A single broken fuel pump grounds their helicopters. A few cut wires silence their radios. Most importantly, they do not understand Vietnam. To them, we are all slant-eyes, primitives to be civilized or enemies to be killed.

The French at least knew us—our language, our culture, our ways of thinking. They learned over decades which Vietnamese to trust, which to fear. These Americans seem to think dollars can replace understanding. They build giant PX stores while our agents run the black market. They hire Vietnamese workers without checking families' political connections. They speak of friendship while building walls between themselves and the people.

Our cadres report increasing opportunities for recruitment. Each new bar district creates dozens of angry fathers. Each field destroyed for their runways dispossesses farmers who then turn to us. Each village relocated for their security brings us new supporters. The Americans' very presence does our political work for us.

Their "strategic hamlet" program copies French failures. They think barbed wire and watchtowers can separate guerrillas from villagers, never understanding that we are the villagers. In one hamlet near Da Nang, they proudly announced that no Viet Cong could enter. Our local commander lives there—he assembled the defense committee.

Even their efforts to help work in our favor. They build schools, but teach American values that offend traditional families. They give medicine to villages, but humiliate respected healers. They hire young women as clerks and translators, but create scandals that drive their brothers to our cause. Every solution creates new problems they cannot see.

Let them build their great bases. Let them think their metal and concrete can control Vietnam. We have learned patience from centuries of resistance. The Chinese came with great armies—we outlasted them. The Mongols came with their hordes—we defeated them. The French came with their technology—we drove them out. The Americans are simply the latest to underestimate Vietnam.

Our Party leaders tell us to study these new enemies carefully. So we watch and learn. Their helicopters are dangerous, but follow predictable patterns. Their jets are powerful, but cannot distinguish friend from foe. Their infantry is strong, but moves so slowly, so blindly through our countryside. Each patrol is like a blind giant, dangerous but easily avoided.

Most interesting is their belief that wars are won by killing enemies and holding territory. They do not understand that revolution is in the minds of the people. While they build bases and count bodies, we build networks and spread ideas. They think Vietnam is a military problem to be solved. We know it is a political struggle to be won.

One of our supporters works as a barber near their base. He says the Americans talk constantly about "light at the end of the tunnel." They do not realize they are building their own tunnel—one that leads only deeper into Vietnam. Like the French, they will learn too late that Vietnam is a trap for foreign armies—the stronger they are, the more deeply they become entangled.

The Party orders us to be patient. Let them build. Let them think their wealth and weapons can buy victory. Time is our ally, the land our friend, the people our strength. When the moment comes, they will learn what the French learned—no foreign army, however strong, can defeat a people fighting for their own soil.

Chapter 38
The Master Sees Giants

The Thoughts of Confucius Upon Viewing Vietnam, Year of the Snake (1965)

I, who taught of harmony between Heaven and Earth, return again to this troubled land. Thirty-five years have passed since my last observation, and I scarcely recognize the country I see. The French masters have gone, but greater powers now stride across Vietnam like giants, careless of what they trample.

The Americans come not as colonizers but as saviors, which makes them more dangerous. They build not mansions like the French, but entire cities of metal and concrete. Their machines transform the landscape—mountains carved for airfields, forests cleared for bases, rice paddies paved for highways. Even the sky belongs to them, filled with their thundering metal birds.

In Da Nang, I watch young Americans giving candy to children. The soldiers mean well, but their generosity carries the same message as French guns—submit to us, learn from us, be like us. They cannot see that every gift creates obligation, every favor demands return. Did I not teach that it is better to learn from the humble than to accept bounty from the mighty?

Most troubling is how they remake Vietnam in their image. Their PX stores sell American dreams. Their radios play American music. Their money turns farmers into laborers, scholars into servants, daughters into bar girls. They call this progress, never understanding that a society's strength lies not in its wealth but in its bonds of obligation and respect.

At a village meeting, I observe young cadres from the North preaching revolution while American advisors nearby speak of democracy. Both sides quote my teachings, yet neither understands. When I spoke of righteous governance, did I not emphasize that rulers must first understand those they would rule?

The Americans bring their own war gods—technology, firepower, logistics. Their bases rise like alien cities, their helicopters swarm like angry wasps, their jets tear holes in the sky. They think these metal dragons will win them victory. They do not see that Vietnam's strength has always been bamboo, not steel—bending with the storm but never breaking.

In Saigon's streets, young Vietnamese wear American clothes, speak American slang, dream American dreams. Yet in their homes, ancestral tablets still watch from shadowed altars. The old ways do not die easily. Did I not teach that a people's character is like a deep river—the surface may be stirred by foreign winds, but the depths maintain their course?

Most painful is the splitting of families. Brother fights brother, uncle suspects nephew, father fears son. When I taught of filial piety and family loyalty, could I have imagined a war that would turn such sacred bonds into weapons? In one home, I saw an ancestral altar divided—some tablets facing north, others south. Even the dead must now choose sides.

The Americans believe they fight communism, but they really battle something older—Vietnam's desperate desire to find its own way. They cannot understand a people who would rather rule themselves poorly than be ruled well by others. Their weapons can destroy armies but cannot defeat ideas. Their dollars can buy allies but cannot purchase loyalty.

In the countryside, I watch farmers bow to passing American patrols while their sons fight with the Viet Cong. This is not duplicity but survival—the wisdom of centuries teaching that foreign powers come and go, but the land remains. Did I not say that the superior man bends like grass in the wind, yet remains rooted in his beliefs?

When I first observed this land, I saw French ambition threatening Vietnamese traditions. When I returned, I saw colonial power crushing ancient ways. Now I see something more profound—not just a war for territory or ideology, but a struggle for Vietnam's soul. The Americans may win battles with their machines, but can they win hearts with their wealth? The communists may promise justice, but can equality replace tradition?

As night falls over this troubled land, I hear the thunder of American guns mixing with the distant sound of temple gongs. The old and new Vietnam clash like storm winds over a troubled sea. And I wonder: When these foreign giants tire of their war games and depart, what will remain of the Vietnam I first knew? What new society will emerge from these fires of transformation?

Perhaps that is the true test facing Vietnam—not choosing between North and South, between communism and capitalism, between East and West, but finding a way to preserve its essence while swimming in these foreign seas.

Let those who would reshape Vietnam learn this truth: A people's spirit is not changed by force or wealth, by guns or gifts. It changes only when it chooses to change, and even then, the old ways flow like underground rivers beneath the new.

For now, I can only watch as giants battle across this ancient land, their feet trampling centuries of tradition. May Heaven grant

Vietnam the wisdom to endure these storms, and the strength to remain itself in the midst of transformation.

Chapter 39

Thunder Rolling North

From the Combat Diary of Captain James "Vegas" Morrison
F-105 Thunderchief Pilot
355th Tactical Fighter Wing
March-July 1965

They tell us we're making history—first sustained bombing campaign against North Vietnam. From my cockpit at 20,000 feet, history looks like tiny black flowers blooming in the jungle below. Russian-made AA guns throw up rivers of red tracers. The North Vietnamese are learning fast. Every mission gets hotter.

Today we hit a munitions depot near Vinh. My wingman took a hit in his left wing but made it back to base. The brass says these strikes will break Hanoi's will to fight. Someone should tell that to the AA gunners—their will seems pretty unbroken to me.

We pilots have a joke: "We're going to bomb them back to the Stone Age—one bicycle at a time." Because that's what we often end up hitting—bicycle convoys carrying supplies down the Ho Chi Minh Trail. A single bike can carry 500 pounds of rice or ammunition. Multiply that by thousands of bikes, all moving at night, all hidden by triple-canopy jungle.

Colonel gave us a pep talk about strategic impact. Every bridge we destroy, every depot we hit, every truck we nail supposedly weakens the enemy's ability to support the Viet Cong in the South. But the next day, the targets are rebuilt. The supplies move by different routes. The war goes on.

Last week we bombed the same bridge three times in four days. The North Vietnamese repair crews are getting as good at rebuilding as we are at destroying. It's become almost routine—we bomb, they rebuild, we bomb again. Like some deadly dance where both partners know the steps.

Lost Baker today. Direct hit from a SA-2 missile. Never saw his chute. The Russian advisers up North are earning their pay—their air defense network grows deadlier by the week. Our ECM gear can't keep up with their radar improvements. Each mission is a roll of the dice.

The politicians put more restrictions on us than the enemy does. Can't hit this, can't bomb that. Have to use this attack angle, can't fly on these days. Meanwhile, the North Vietnamese adapt and improve. Their air defense system looks like a spider web on our intel maps—getting thicker and deadlier every week.

Sometimes I wonder what the boys in the trenches down South think of our efforts. Are we helping them? The brass shows us photos of destroyed targets, charts of diminished supply flow, graphs of bombing effectiveness. But Charlie keeps fighting. The supplies keep moving. The war keeps grinding on.

We're the most technologically advanced air force in history, dropping more bombs than we did in World War II, yet we're fighting an enemy who can melt into the jungle and survive on a handful of rice. Something's not adding up.

Tonight in the officers' club, Williams from the 388th said something that stuck with me: "We're playing chess. They're playing go. Different games, different victory conditions." I'm not sure what that means, but it feels true.

Every morning I strap into my Thud (F-105), armed with the latest smart bombs and electronic countermeasures. Below me, men in black pajamas push bicycles through the jungle at night, living on rice and determination. Our technology against their tenacity. Our bombs against their belief.

Lost another one today—Johnson took a 37mm round through his cockpit. His wingman said the canopy just disappeared in a red mist. Back in the ready room, his chair stays empty. Tomorrow we'll fly his slot, bomb his targets, roll his dice with the SA-2s and the AA guns.

The brass keeps telling us we're winning, wearing them down, degrading their capability. But from my cockpit, I see supply trucks moving at night, bridges rising from their ruins, AA guns multiplying like deadly mushrooms. Most telling: no matter how many missions we fly, the enemy's resistance grows stronger, not weaker.

Here's what they don't tell you about strategic bombing: it's personal. Every time I roll in on a target, someone down there is trying to kill me. Not some faceless enemy, but a skilled professional who's getting better at his job. We're the world's most sophisticated air force, and we're being fought to a standstill by determined men with second-hand Soviet weapons.

Tomorrow we hit the same railyard we bombed last week. The craters will be filled, the tracks repaired, the AA guns waiting. We'll brief the mission, study the photos, plan our attack runs. Some of us won't come back. The survivors will file reports claiming X percent of the target destroyed. And the dance goes on.

They say Thunder is rolling North, but some nights, lying in my bunk listening to the distant sound of choppers heading South, I wonder who's really winning this war of attrition—the side with the bombs, or the side with the bicycles?

Chapter 40

The Dying Jungle

I am the jungle of A Luoi Valley. For ten thousand years, I have cradled life in my green embrace. My roots remember the first human footsteps, my leaves whisper tales of centuries past. I have sheltered tigers in my shadows, sung with a million birds, hidden entire armies beneath my canopy.

The Vietnamese call me "mother of all things." Through monsoons and droughts, through peace and war, I have been their protector. My vines fed them when crops failed. My plants healed their sick. My thick canopy sheltered their fighters—against the Chinese, the French, all who would claim this land.

When the first Americans came, I did what I had always done—wrapped my children in green shadows, confused their enemies with my twisting paths, offered sanctuary in my deepest places. Their machines could not find my hidden trails. Their bombs could not penetrate my layers of life.

Then came the strange rain.

At first, it seemed merely odd—mist falling from silver birds, rainbow droplets clinging to leaves. But this was not monsoon rain that feeds life. This was something else. Something that burned.

My leaves began to curl, brown creeping across their green faces like age spots. Birds fell silent. Animals fled, or tried to flee. Some drank from my poisoned streams and died convulsing. Others grew sick slowly, their offspring born twisted and wrong.

I tried to heal myself as I had always done. When storms toppled trees, I grew new ones. When fire scarred my skin, I covered the burns with fresh growth. But this poison went deeper. It killed my roots, corrupted my soil, turned my green blood to death.

The people who lived in my embrace began to sicken. Mothers gave birth to children with strange deformities. Old men developed weeping sores. The rainbow poison had no mercy—it killed slowly, inexorably, passed its curse from parent to child.

My ancient friends, the Dao and Ta Oi peoples whose ancestors I had sheltered for generations, abandoned their villages. The rainbow death followed them. It lived in the soil, in the water, in the very air. They had survived wars, famines, floods—but they could not survive this invisible killer.

Now I stand dying, my once-green branches bare against the sky. Where a million lives once sang beneath my canopy, silence spreads like another kind of death. The birds do not return. The tigers are gone. Even the insects, who survived all previous wars, have disappeared from my poisoned realm.

The Americans call it Agent Orange. They say it was necessary to expose their enemies, to defoliate my protective cover. Perhaps they did not know their rainbow death would linger for generations. Perhaps they did not understand that killing a jungle means killing all it shelters, all it sustains, all it might nurture for centuries to come.

I watch the young shoots that struggle to grow in my poisoned soil. They emerge twisted, sickly, bearing the curse of the rainbow death in their very cells. The people who return to farm plant their rice, but the land remembers. Their children will remember too, in their blood, in their bones.

A thousand bombs could not kill me. Ten thousand years of storms could not break me. But this silent poison, this rainbow death, has done what no army could do. I am dying, not just for now, but for generations to come. The silver birds have stolen not just my present life, but my future ones.

At night, when the burning mists have cleared, I hear the ghosts of all I sheltered—the tigers' roar, the gibbons' song, the laughter of children now grown silent. I was the mother of all things, and now I watch my children die.

They say wars end. Leaders sign papers, soldiers go home, wounds heal. But I will carry these scars forever. My soil will remember. My streams will remember. The rainbow death will whisper in my branches long after those who sent the silver birds have forgotten my name.

I am the jungle of A Luoi Valley. I have witnessed a thousand seasons of death and rebirth. But this death is different. This is the death not just of my present, but of all the futures I might have nurtured, all the lives I might have sheltered, all the stories I might have witnessed.

The Vietnamese say the land endures while armies come and go. But some armies leave wounds that never heal, poisons that never fade. I am the jungle, and I am dying. Not just for today, but for all the tomorrows that will never be.

Chapter 41

Just Another Day

From the War Journal of Specialist James Walker
25th Infantry Division
Tay Ninh Province, 1967

Another search and destroy mission. Another day humping the boonies looking for an enemy who sees us before we see them. We protect the villages by destroying them. We save civilians by making them homeless. We win hearts and minds through body counts. Charlie may be crazy, but at least his war makes sense.

Today started like they all do—up at dawn, check weapons, swallow something from a C-rat can. Lieutenant Reynolds gave us the usual pep talk about strategic hamlets and pacification. Same speech, different jungle. The new guys still take notes. Those of us who've been here a while just check our ammo.

Sergeant Garcia called me "the professor" when he caught me writing between guard shifts. "College boy keeping a diary?" he smirked. But he's the one who taught me to record everything—not just firefights and body counts, but the look in a villager's eyes when we torch their hootch, the smell of jungle rot and burning shit, the sound of incoming mortar rounds. "Somebody needs to tell the truth about this mess," he said.

We found a tunnel complex around noon. The usual drill—send the tunnel rats down to check for Charlie, weapons, rice caches. I watched Jimmy Carson disappear into that black hole with just a .45 and a flashlight. He's nineteen. Last week he was flipping burgers in Kansas. Now he crawls through Viet Cong tunnels, where death can come from any shadow.

Carson found maps, ammo, medical supplies. Also a nursery—little sleeping mats, children's toys. The VC don't separate military from civilian like we do. Their whole society goes underground while we stomp around above, pretending to control territory we only hold in daylight.

The village nearby was "friendly"—meaning they smiled to our faces. An old mama-san offered us rice. The same woman probably feeds Charlie when we're gone. Can't blame her. We come and go. The VC are here always. Someone wrote on our barracks wall: "Hearts and minds is a math problem. VC terrorism plus GI stupidity equals Vietnamese neutrality."

Lost Peterson today. Sniper got him during a piss call. One minute he's bitching about the heat, the next he's sprawled in the mud with half his head missing. We called in gunships, burned down half a klick of jungle. Maybe we got the sniper, maybe not. Doesn't matter. There's always another sniper, another tunnel, another village that smiles in daylight and shoots at night.

The new lieutenant wants body count. Army runs on statistics—x number of enemy killed, y number of weapons captured, z number of villages pacified. But Charlie doesn't play by our numbers. We kill ten, twenty more take their place. We destroy one tunnel network, they build two more. Even their dead mock us—half the corpses we count disappear before the brass can verify.

Found a booby trap the hard way—trip wire connected to an American claymore mine. They use our own weapons against us. Medic says Thompson will keep his leg, probably won't dance again. The real bitch is knowing the mine was ours, supplied to the ARVN, sold to the VC, replanted for GIs to find.

Back at base, hot food and armed forces radio playing Aretha Franklin. News says we're winning, peace talks coming soon. Same news we heard last year. Meanwhile, Charlie keeps fighting, villagers keep smiling and lying, politicians keep counting bodies, and we keep humping through the jungle looking for a war we can't find and can't win.

Garcia says I think too much. "War ain't supposed to make sense," he tells me. "Just do your job and try to stay alive." He's probably right. But I keep writing, keep watching, keep wondering—what's the truth about this war? The official truth in Stars and Stripes? The grunt truth in the mud? The village truth behind those smiling lies?

Maybe there is no truth, just different angles on the same madness. We patrol in daylight, they own the night. We build fortified hamlets, they dig tunnels beneath them. We count bodies, they count time. Even the land switches sides—solid ground one minute, punji pit the next.

Tomorrow we do it again. Another search and destroy, another strategic hamlet, another body count. The war machine needs feeding—reports to file, statistics to quote, territory to claim. But we all know the real score: Charlie isn't fighting our kind of war. He doesn't need to win battles or hold ground. He just needs to keep us off balance, keep us jumping at shadows, keep us spending blood and treasure in a fight we don't understand.

Peterson's replacement arrives tomorrow. FNG from Alabama, probably still believes in hearts and minds, body counts, light at the end of the tunnel. He'll learn. We all learn eventually. This isn't a war of territory or body counts or hearts and minds. It's a war of wills. And you can't bomb a will, or burn it, or make it switch sides.

Just another day in the Nam. Pass the ammunition.

Chapter 42

What We Became

Private Michael Collins
Charlie Company, 1st Battalion, 20th Infantry Regiment
My Lai, March 16, 1968
Written in 1970

They say confession cleanses the soul. I've been to three priests since My Lai. None could grant absolution. Not for what I did—I never pulled a trigger. For what I didn't do. For what I watched happen and did nothing to stop.

It started like any other sweep. Another village suspected of harboring VC. Another chance to avenge our losses from mines and snipers. But something was different that morning. The officers' briefing had an edge to it. "Every living thing," Captain Medina said. "Animals, chickens, everything."

No one directly said "kill civilians." They didn't have to.

The first shots caught me by surprise—old men gunned down in doorways, women running with children in their arms, falling together. I stood frozen, watching my friends, guys I shared cigarettes with, guys who sent money home to their mothers, turn into something monstrous.

A woman ran past me holding a baby. Behind her, Roberts raised his M-16. I opened my mouth to shout but no sound came. The woman fell. The baby lay crying on her back until someone silenced it with a pistol shot.

They threw grenades into shelters full of women and children. Shot farmers in their fields. Gunned down entire families trying to run away. Some begged in Vietnamese. Some held up their children, trying to appeal to our humanity. But we had lost our humanity somewhere between boot camp and that morning.

I watched it all. That's my crime. I watched. I didn't participate, but I didn't try to stop it either. What do you call someone who watches children die and does nothing? What's the moral difference between pulling the trigger and watching the trigger being pulled?

Hours later, the shooting finally stopped. The village was silent except for the moans of the dying. Smoke from burning huts drifted across fields littered with bodies—over 500 dead, most of them women, children, and old men.

We found no weapons. No VC. Just slaughtered civilians and our own lost souls.

That night, back at base, nobody talked about what happened. We cleaned our weapons, wrote letters home, acted like it was just another day in the war. But something had changed. We couldn't look each other in the eye. We knew what we had become.

They say war is hell. But hell is populated by devils. What happened at My Lai was humans choosing to become devils. I watched that transformation—saw good men, decent men, become monsters. Saw others, like me, become cowards in the face of evil.

When the investigation finally came, most kept quiet. Code of silence. Protect the unit. But the truth haunted us. It came out in nightmares, in drinking binges, in broken marriages and ruined lives. You can't witness something like My Lai without it changing you forever.

Thompson, the helicopter pilot who finally stopped the killing by threatening to shoot his fellow Americans, is the only real hero in this story. He chose humanity over unit loyalty. Chose moral courage over following orders. While I stood watching, he acted.

Now, two years later, I still hear the shots, the screams, the silence that followed. I see the bodies in ditches, the burning huts, the faces of men I once called friends as they committed unspeakable acts. But mostly I see myself, standing frozen, watching it happen.

They say war brings out both the best and worst in men. At My Lai, we saw only the worst. Some fired the shots. Some gave the orders. Some, like me, just watched. All of us lost something that day—not just our innocence or humanity, but our right to think of ourselves as good people.

This is my confession: I was there. I watched. I did nothing. The priests say God may forgive me. I don't believe I'll ever forgive myself.

Chapter 43

When Night Became Day

Dual Accounts of the 1968 Tet Offensive

(From the captured diary of Nguyen Van Duc
Viet Cong Sapper, Saigon Cell)
January 30, 1968
Eve of Tet

For months we prepared, moving weapons into Saigon piece by piece. A mortar tube hidden in a flower vendor's cart. Ammunition concealed in funeral urns. AK-47s buried in cemetery plots. Right under the Americans' noses, we built an arsenal in their "secure" capital.

My cell shelters in a sympathizer's house near the U.S. Embassy. Fifteen of us packed into a basement, studying diagrams, synchronizing watches. Tomorrow, while Saigon celebrates Tet, we emerge from the shadows. For years we've been the night—invisible, patient, deadly. Tomorrow we own the day.

January 31, 1968
0300 Hours

The city sleeps, dreaming of holiday feasts and family gatherings. In an hour, those dreams become nightmares. Our orders are precise—breach the Embassy walls, seize the grounds, hold until relief forces arrive. A suicide mission, but one that will shake American confidence forever.

Never seen Saigon so quiet. Then the mortars begin—our signal. Across the city, thousands of us rise from our hiding places. We are everywhere—the drinks server at the officers' club, the barber who shaves American necks, the clerk who polishes their boots. Now the servants become the masters.

(From the combat log of Sergeant Mike Cohen
Military Police, U.S. Embassy Guard Detail)
January 31, 1968
0245 Hours

Quiet night. Too quiet. Even the usual street noise is dead. Something feels wrong. Called it in but the duty officer just reminded me it's Tet—everything's supposed to be quiet.

0315 Hours

Jesus Christ. The whole city's exploding. Mortars landing everywhere. Report VC shooting up the BOQ, the ammo dump, the airfield. Radio's going crazy with reports. Every guard post calling in contact.

Wait—movement at the Embassy wall. Holy shit -

Nguyen Van Duc

The explosion breaches the wall right on schedule. We pour
through the gap, firing at the guard posts. Americans totally surprised—still in their underwear, grabbing weapons. We push toward the main building. Already I've lost three comrades, but we
keep moving. The Embassy is the symbol of American power—its
capture will prove they can be beaten.

Sergeant Cohen

They're inside the compound. Never seen anything like it—VC
in black pajamas shooting up the most secure building in Saigon.
Called for reinforcements but the whole city's under attack. We're
on our own.

Marines on the roof are giving them hell. But these guys keep
coming. Suicide charges right into our fire. They really think they
can take the Embassy. Maybe they can.

Nguyen Van Duc

Noon now. We've lost half our cell but still hold parts of the
compound. The relief force never came—heard later they were
caught in ambushes across the city. No matter. We've already won
by proving we can hit them anywhere.

From my position behind a burned-out car, I see American
gunships circling, troops rushing in. They'll retake the Embassy,
but can never recapture their lost illusion of invulnerability. All
across Saigon, all across Vietnam, we rise from the shadows. The

Americans thought they were winning. Today we show them how wrong they were.

Sergeant Cohen

Finally secured the Embassy grounds at 1500. Inside is a slaughterhouse. The VC who got into the building fought to the last man. Had to kill them room by room. Never seen such determination.

Looking out over Saigon now. Smoke everywhere. Gunfire echoes from every district. Reports say we're under attack across the whole country—every major city, every provincial capital. How the hell did we miss this? How did they infiltrate so many fighters, so many weapons?

Just heard Westmoreland on the radio claiming this is a sign of desperation, that the VC are throwing away their forces in one last gamble. Maybe. But something tells me this changes everything. They didn't just attack—they shattered our confidence, exposed our vulnerabilities, showed the world they can hit us anywhere.

We'll win this battle. Already pushing them back across the city. But the cost...and the realization that all our talk of "secure areas" and "pacified provinces" was self-delusion...

Nguyen Van Duc

Night falls. Most of my cell is dead. The survivors slip away through sewers and back alleys. Our attacks across Vietnam are being crushed by American firepower. But we knew this would happen. Military victory was never the goal.

The real victory is in the American newspapers, the shocked faces of their soldiers, the collapse of their illusions. They thought they were winning a war of attrition. We showed them they're losing the war of wills.

Dawn approaches. Time to disappear back into the shadows. We lost many fighters today, but killed something even more valuable—American faith in their leaders, their strategy, their ability to win this war.

Let them keep their Embassy. We've captured something far more precious—doubt in their minds, fear in their hearts. The American giant bleeds. Now their own people will begin to ask the questions that will bring them home.

Chapter 44

The Night of March 31

From the Private Diary of President Lyndon B. Johnson
March 31, 1968

They're waiting for my speech now—the networks, the press, the American people. They expect me to talk about Vietnam, about peace negotiations, about troop levels. They don't know I'm about to drop a bomb bigger than anything we've thrown at Hanoi.

Bird's the only one who knows my decision. Even now she's begging me to reconsider. "You're letting them win," she says. "The critics, the protesters, the media vultures." Maybe she's right. But when I lay in bed last night staring at the ceiling, listening to the grandfather clock tick away my presidency, I knew I couldn't take another year of this.

Every morning I study the casualty reports—young American boys dead in a war I can't explain anymore. Every afternoon I read the intelligence briefings—always promising light at the end of the tunnel, but the tunnel keeps getting longer and darker. Every night I look in the mirror and see myself aging a year each week.

Tet broke something in me. Not just the shock of it, but the realization that everything we'd been telling the American people was a lie. Westmoreland kept promising victory was around the corner. The CIA kept saying the Viet Cong were on their last legs. Then suddenly they're inside our embassy, attacking every major city, making us look like fools or liars. Maybe both.

I remember what my daddy used to say: "When you've lost your credibility, son, you've lost everything." Looking at the polls, reading the newspapers, watching the protesters—I've lost it all. They don't believe me anymore. Hell, some days I don't believe myself.

The worst part is the dreams. Dead soldiers parade through my sleep, asking why. Vietnamese children burned by napalm. American boys in body bags. I wake up sweating, reach for the phone to order another bombing halt, then remember it won't make any difference. Nothing seems to make a difference anymore.

Bobby Kennedy's running now. Even Clean Gene McCarthy beats me in the polls. My own party wants me gone. Me—who passed Civil Rights, who launched the Great Society, who tried to build the Great American Dream. But none of that matters. I'll go down in history as the Vietnam President, the one who couldn't win and couldn't get out.

The speech is ready. My hands shake every time I read it. "I shall not seek, and I will not accept, the nomination of my party for another term as your President." Fourteen words that end a lifetime of political ambition.

Maybe this is cowardice. Maybe I should stay and fight. But I keep thinking of that old preacher in Johnson City who said, "Sometimes the most powerful thing a man can do is admit he's powerless."

They say power is addictive. They're wrong. It's not the power that hooks you—it's the belief that you can use it to do good. I really thought I could build a Great Society at home while fighting communism abroad. Instead, Vietnam is eating my presidency alive, destroying everything I hoped to build.

The networks are ready. In five minutes, I'll walk into the Oval Office and destroy my own presidency to save it. Or maybe to save myself. I don't even know anymore.

Bird just brought me a glass of water, touched my shoulder. She knows what this costs me. Knows that with these fourteen words, I'm murdering my own dreams. But she also knows I haven't slept through the night since Tet. Haven't laughed since I can't remember when. Haven't believed my own words in too long.

The door's opening. Time to go. History will judge whether I'm doing the right thing. But tonight, for the first time in months, I think I might sleep without seeing dead boys in my dreams.

God help me. God help us all.

Chapter 45

Dinner is Served

From Personal Notes of Colonel Richard Andrews
Top Secret B-52 Squadron Commander
March 1969

Another "breakfast" mission tonight. That's the code—breakfast, lunch, dinner—for bombing targets we're not supposed to hit in a country we're not supposed to be bombing. The crews joke about it: "Time to feed the neutrals." But there's nothing funny about falsifying coordinates, lying to Congress, violating international law.

The orders come straight from the top. President Nixon and Kissinger want the "Menu" series kept totally black. Our flight plans show targets in South Vietnam. Only after takeoff do we give the crews the real coordinates—targets in Cambodia. After landing, we doctor the logs, destroy the real records, create a paper trail that never happened.

Tonight's target is a suspected North Vietnamese base camp just inside Cambodia. "Suspected" because our intelligence is shaky. Could be a military depot. Could be a village. Could be nothing but jungle. Hard to know when we're dropping high explosives from 30,000 feet in the dark.

Captain Reynolds asked me a hard question at briefing: "Sir, if these strikes are legitimate, why are we lying about them?" I gave him the official answer about diplomatic sensitivities, neutral countries, national security. The words tasted like ashes in my mouth.

Three years ago, I wouldn't have believed I'd be part of something like this. Planning strikes based on coordinates we can't verify, against targets we can't confirm, in a country we're not at war with. The dead are just as dead whether we admit to killing them or not.

The weather report shows clear skies over the target area. No way to call it off for weather. Some nights I pray for storms, anything to avoid sending young men to drop death on people whose only crime is living on the wrong side of an invisible line.

My crew chief understands what we're doing. "Menu is served," he says bitterly as the planes take off. "Come back for seconds tomorrow night." He lost a brother in Khe Sanh. Says at least that was an honest fight, not this midnight murder.

The planes return. Pilots report secondary explosions—could mean ammunition dumps, could mean fuel storage, could mean farmer's petroleum tanks. Could mean anything. We'll never know. The Cambodians can't protest strikes that officially never happened.

Post-mission paperwork is the worst. Creating fake flight plans. Drafting false reports. Teaching young officers to lie convincingly. This isn't what any of us signed up for. But orders are orders, and these come from the Commander-in-Chief himself.

Late at night, alone with my thoughts, I wonder what this is doing to us—not just as soldiers, but as a nation. When did we become people who bomb neutral countries in secret? When did we start measuring honor by our ability to hide the truth?

The crews are starting to crack. Not obviously—they're too professional for that. But I see it in their eyes, hear it in their voices. They joined to fight for their country openly, proudly. Instead, they're flying secret missions they can't talk about, dropping bombs they can't acknowledge, fighting a war that officially doesn't exist.

Tomorrow we do it again. Another "menu" selection, another target that isn't there, another mission that never happened. The lies pile up like bomb craters in the Cambodian jungle.

They say truth is the first casualty of war. But this is different. This isn't hiding the truth—it's creating a whole false reality. We're not just deceiving the enemy or the public. We're trying to deceive history itself.

Latest intel suggests the North Vietnamese are just moving deeper into Cambodia, setting up new bases, new supply routes. We're not stopping them—just pushing them further in, spreading the war like a cancer into another country.

The crew boards for tonight's mission. Young men who trust their commanders to tell them the truth, who believe they're fighting an honest war. I watch them suit up, climb into their planes, take off into the darkness. They'll drop their bombs exactly as ordered, precisely on target. Then they'll come back and lie about where they've been.

This is how empires fall, I think—not from external enemies, but from the rot within. From the small corruptions that lead to larger ones. From believing that the end justifies any means. From midnight bombings that never happened.

God forgive us. History won't.

Chapter 46

What the Camera Sees

From the Working Journal of David Cohen
Senior Producer, CBS Evening News
1969

They tell us to be objective, but the camera has its own truth. Tonight we're editing footage from Hamburger Hill—American boys dying to take a mountain they'll abandon next week. The official briefing calls it a "significant tactical victory." But the camera shows dead 19-year-olds in body bags. You can't spin that.

My desk is buried in footage that will never air. An American patrol burning a village. A South Vietnamese officer executing a prisoner. Wounded soldiers screaming for morphine. "Too graphic," the executives say. "The public isn't ready." But they've been saying that for years, and the public isn't buying it anymore.

Walter's been different since Tet. We all have. For years we played along—reported the official story, showed the sanitized version. Then suddenly the Viet Cong were inside our embassy, and everything we'd been telling the American people was exposed as fantasy. The day Walter declared the war unwinnable on air, something broke. The emperor had no clothes, and we finally said it.

Just got off the phone with our Saigon bureau. They're tracking a story about falsified body counts, but the military's stonewalling. Five years ago we would have backed off. Now we push harder. The official lies don't work anymore—not after Tet, not after My Lai, not after years of "light at the end of the tunnel."

Today's feed shows anti-war protesters at the Pentagon. Not longhaired hippies this time—middle-class families, veterans, ordinary Americans. We'll run it tonight. The war's critics aren't fringe elements anymore. They're the mainstream, and our coverage reflects that.

The military still feeds us their version—maps with arrows showing territory controlled, statistics proving we're winning, generals promising victory. But our cameras show the truth: the same territory being taken again and again, the same battles being fought over and over, the same body bags coming home.

Young photographer just back from the field broke down in my office. His footage showed an American patrol gunning down civilians who didn't stop at a checkpoint. Clear violation of rules of engagement. But one soldier told him, "Charlie killed my buddy yesterday. Today everyone's Charlie." We can't air it—too graphic. But the photographer's hands shook as he described it. "This isn't what we're supposed to be," he kept saying.

The shift happened slowly, then all at once. First a few reporters started questioning the official line. Then more. Then Walter. Now even the most hawkish newspapers are asking hard questions. We're not anti-war—we're just showing what's happening. The camera doesn't lie, even when everyone else does.

Latest polls show 70% of Americans think the war was a mistake. They're not seeing anything new—just finally believing what they see. The burned children, the napalmed villages, the endless body bags. It was always there in our footage, between the lines of our reports. Now people are ready to look.

My son asks why I don't run more positive stories about the war. "Surely our boys are doing good things too," he says. They are. We show those stories—medical aid, school building, food distribution. But you can't balance a shot of a dead child with a shot of a soldier handing out candy. Some truths outweigh others.

Tonight's broadcast leads with Hamburger Hill. We'll show what we can—not the worst of it, but enough. Enough to keep chipping away at the official story. Enough to show the truth the camera sees. Enough to help end this.

The Pentagon called to complain about yesterday's coverage. Said we're undermining morale, helping the enemy. I asked them about the false body counts, the bombed villages, the civilian casualties. They hung up. They still think it's about propaganda versus counter-propaganda. They don't understand—the camera has its own truth, and that truth is finally being seen.

The turning point wasn't any single story or image. It was the slow accumulation of truth, the steady erosion of official lies. The camera showed what was happening, and finally, people believed their eyes instead of their leaders.

We're not protesters or activists. We're witnesses. The camera is our testimony. And finally, America is ready to see what it shows.

Chapter 47

Four Dead in Ohio

Three Voices from Kent State
May 4, 1970

Sarah Mitchell, Student
Sophomore, Art Major

We were angry about Cambodia. Another escalation, another lie. The ROTC building burned Saturday night—not by us, but they blamed us anyway. The Guard came Sunday, strutting around our campus like an occupying army. Their rifles didn't scare us. This was Kent State, not Vietnam.

Monday dawned clear and warm. Perfect protest weather. We gathered on the Commons despite the ban. Someone threw rocks at the Guard—stupid, but they were only rocks. They had M-1 rifles. We were students with books in our backpacks, not Viet Cong with AK-47s.

When they fired tear gas, we threw it back. It felt like a game—them advancing, us retreating, then pushing forward again. The bell in Taylor Hall tolled noon. I remember thinking: "In an hour, I have Art History."

Then the shots. Not blanks. Not warning shots. Real bullets cutting through the spring air. Students falling. For a moment, nobody moved. It seemed impossible—American soldiers wouldn't shoot American students. But they did.

Allison lay face down in the parking lot, blood pooling around her. She wasn't even protesting—just walking to class. I keep seeing her there, notebooks scattered around her body like broken wings.

Private James Cooper
Ohio National Guard

They called us in after the ROTC fire. Most of us were part-timers—factory workers, office clerks, teachers. None of us wanted to be there. The students taunted us, called us pigs, fascists, baby killers. We hadn't slept in 24 hours.

Monday, they wouldn't disperse. Rocks and bottles flew. Tear gas didn't work—the wind kept blowing it back at us. We were tired, scared, angry. Someone yelled they had a sniper. Others heard shots. Maybe we imagined it. Everything was chaos.

When the order came to get into firing position, it felt like a dream. These were American kids, not enemy soldiers. But they kept coming at us. The rocks kept flying. Someone screamed "Shoot!" I still don't know who.

Twenty-eight of us fired. Sixty-seven rounds in 13 seconds. I don't know if my bullets hit anyone. I pray they didn't. But I'll always remember the silence after—just the spent shell casings rolling on the asphalt and someone crying "They're killing us."

Professor Robert Warren
History Department

I was in my office when I heard the shots. My window overlooks the Commons. For a moment, I thought it was a demonstration tactic—blanks or firecrackers. Then I saw students falling. Real blood. Real bodies. Real bullets in a peaceful Ohio town.

The campus became a battlefield. Students running, screaming, trying to help the wounded. Guards advancing with fixed bayonets. Tear gas drifting across the parking lot where Jeffrey Miller lay dead, his blood running between the painted parking lines.

My Vietnam veteran students recognized the sound immediately - M-1 rifles on semi-automatic. "Just like Nam," one said, his face white with shock. "Except Charlie shoots back."

The university closed immediately. Students were ordered to leave campus. But how do you close a college after something like this? How do you explain American troops killing American students on American soil?

We faculty had already been divided over the war, over student protests, over our role as educators in a time of conflict. Now we faced harder questions: What happens when war comes home? When the divisions in Vietnam become divisions in Ohio?

(Later that night)

Sarah:

Tonight the campus is empty except for police and Guard patrols. The bloodstains are still visible on the parking lot. Someone laid flowers where Allison fell. Four dead. Nine wounded. All because we dared to question, to protest, to believe we had the right to speak.

They say the shooting only lasted 13 seconds. But those seconds changed everything. The war isn't just "over there" anymore. It's here, on our campus, in our parking lots, in our nightmares.

James:

They've pulled us back to the armory. Nobody's talking much. The officials say we acted properly, that we were threatened. Maybe we were. But I keep seeing those kids falling. Keep wondering: How did we get here? When did American students become the enemy?

My rifle's been taken for ballistics. Maybe they'll tell me if I killed someone. Maybe it's better not to know. My hands won't stop shaking.

Professor Warren:

The press is calling it a massacre. The Governor blames outside agitators. The university administration promises investigation. But the truth is simpler and harder: America's war came home today. The same bullets we've been using in Vietnam found targets in Ohio.

Tomorrow I'll pack up my office—campus is closed "until further notice." But some things can't be closed or packed away. The war has crossed a line. The divisions have deepened. And four young Americans who woke up planning to go to class are dead on their own campus.

God help us all.

Chapter 48

Truths and Consequences

From the Personal Diary of Daniel Ellsberg
RAND Corporation
1971

Another late night at the Xerox machine. Seven thousand pages, each one damning. My back aches, my hands are black with toner, but I can't stop. Every document I copy is another nail in the coffin of official lies.

The guard thinks I'm just another bureaucrat working overtime. If he knew what these papers contain—the systematic deception of Congress and the public, the calculated escalation of an unwinnable war, the cold analysis showing we couldn't succeed even as presidents promised victory.

McNamara commissioned this study himself, then buried it when the truth became too ugly. "The Pentagon Papers"—such a bland name for such explosive content. Year by year, decision by decision, the story of how we deceived ourselves and others, how we committed ourselves to a war we knew we couldn't win.

Patricia helps me organize the copies at home. "You'll go to prison for this," she says. Not a question - a fact. I tell her the same thing I tell myself: some truths are worth prison. Some lies are too dangerous to keep hidden.

Looking at these documents, I remember my own role. Marine Corps officer. Pentagon analyst. Cold warrior. I believed in domino theories and containment strategies. Wrote my share of reports minimizing casualties, maximizing progress. Now I'm trying to undo those lies by exposing even bigger ones.

Today I copied the Gulf of Tonkin section. No attack on August 4th—we knew it then, covered it up, used it to get congressional authorization anyway. How many Americans have died because of that lie? The number haunts me: 50,000 and counting.

Called Neil Sheehan at the New York Times again. He's cautious—knows publishing these papers could mean criminal charges for everyone involved. But he also knows what they represent: irrefutable evidence that four presidents systematically lied about Vietnam.

The hardest part isn't the fear of prison. It's confronting my own complicity. I was there in the Pentagon, saw the deception firsthand, wrote some of the lies myself. Believed I was serving my country. Now I have to ask: What is real service? Following orders or exposing truth?

The papers show it all. Eisenhower preventing the 1956 elections because we knew Ho Chi Minh would win. Kennedy escalating while denying it. Johnson planning bombing campaigns even while campaigning as the peace candidate. Nixon sabotaging peace talks to win the '68 election.

Each page I copy feels like an act of penance. For my own sins, for our collective sins, for a war built on lies. The truth has become my personal Vietnam—a jungle I have to fight through, a weight I have to carry, a burden I can't put down.

Some would call this treason. I call it patriotism. These documents belong to the American people. They paid for this war with their blood and treasure. They deserve to know why their sons died, why their country lied, why their trust was betrayed.

The Times lawyers are nervous. Publication would break new ground—no one has ever published classified documents on this scale before. But these aren't military secrets—they're political secrets. The difference matters. One protects our country; the other protects our leaders from accountability.

Last night I dreamed of burning villages, napalmed children, body bags coming home. Woke up knowing: the lies must end. Not just about specific battles or body counts, but the fundamental lie that we're fighting for freedom, democracy, self-determination. The papers show we've been fighting against all three.

Tomorrow the first batch goes to the Times. No turning back now. My security clearance will be revoked, my career destroyed, my freedom at risk. Small prices to pay for truth. The war has already cost too much—in lives, in honor, in American credibility.

They'll call me traitor, but I can live with that. I can't live with more lies. Can't watch more young Americans die for deceptions documented in these papers. The truth is heavy, but lies are heavier.

History will judge whether I'm right or wrong. But at least it will judge based on truth, not carefully crafted fictions. That's worth whatever comes next.

The copying is almost done. My hands shake as I collate the final pages. Seven thousand pages of evidence. Seven thousand reasons why the war must end. Seven thousand steps toward truth.

God help me. God help us all.

Chapter 49

Teaching Tigers to Fight

From Field Reports of Major David Harrison
U.S. Army Advisory Team 47
Mekong Delta, 1971-72

Another ARVN "victory" today. My Vietnamese counterpart, Captain Nguyen, proudly showed me the body count. What he didn't mention was that his troops only engaged after our gunships softened up the enemy, our artillery boxed them in, and our air support cut off their retreat. Some victory.

This is what Vietnamization looks like on the ground. We're supposed to be teaching them to fight their own war, but how do you teach an army to replace the world's biggest war machine? The ARVN has brave soldiers, but bravery can't replace gunships, artillery, and unlimited air support.

Captain Nguyen is no fool. Over rice wine last night, he said something that chilled me: "You Americans fight with machines. We must fight with men. But our men know you are leaving, while the enemy knows they are staying. How do you calculate such things in your battle plans?"

Today I watched ARVN troops train on our equipment. Some units are excellent—tough, disciplined, ready to fight. Others are hollow shells, their officers more interested in political connections than military competence. The good ones know what's coming. The bad ones are already making escape plans.

The official reports show progress—more ARVN troops trained, more operations conducted independently, more territory under Saigon's control. The reality is messier. Without American air support, many ARVN units won't leave their bases. Without American advisors calling in strikes, they avoid contact with the enemy.

Got the latest "achievements" report from Saigon—all statistics, percentages, metrics of success. Somehow they never mention the ARVN units that evaporate under pressure, the officers who buy their positions, the soldiers who desert with their weapons. Can't blame them. We're asking them to die for a government that may not survive our departure.

My counterpart is brutally honest after a few drinks. "You're teaching us to fight like Americans," he said. "But we're not Americans. We don't have your factories, your technology, your wealth. When you leave, all your methods become useless."

The enemy knows our game. They probe, test, watch. Their propaganda tells ARVN soldiers: "The Americans are abandoning you. But we will still be here." Hard to counter that message when every week another U.S. unit packs up and goes home.

Operation Lam Son 719 showed the truth about Vietnamization. ARVN troops fought bravely but were mauled the moment they lost U.S. air support. Now everyone knows what happens when they fight without American backing. The lesson isn't lost on anyone.

Yesterday I inspected an ARVN ammunition depot. On paper, everything perfect. In reality, half the shells sold on the black market, replaced with empty crates. The colonel in charge shrugged: "After you leave, we'll need money more than ammunition."

My reports get more pessimistic each month. Headquarters keeps bouncing them back for "revision." They want success stories, proof that Vietnamization works. But you can't train an army to fight like Americans without American resources. Can't expect them to hold territory without the massive firepower that let us hold it.

The enemy's strategy is perfect: let us leave, then test the ARVN's will to fight. They know that without U.S. backing, the South's advantages evaporate. Know that every ARVN soldier is asking himself: "Am I fighting for the winning side?"

Dinner with Captain Nguyen tonight. He showed me pictures of his family, talked about sending them to relatives in France. "Just in case," he said. Then: "Your politicians say we're ready to fight our own war. Do they believe their own words?"

The truth is brutal: we're not transferring responsibility—we're transferring blame. When the ARVN collapses, we'll say they failed, not us. They lacked the will to fight, not the means to win. Easier than admitting we built a military that can only fight with resources they'll never have.

Some ARVN units will fight to the death—already have. But an army isn't made of heroes alone. It needs structure, support, belief in victory. How do you instill that while simultaneously withdrawing everything that made victory possible?

Captain Nguyen summed it up: "You taught us to swim by holding us up in the water. Now you'll let go, declare us swimmers, and leave. But the water is deep, and there are sharks, and we never learned to swim without you."

Final evaluation report due tomorrow. I'll write what they want to hear—metrics met, benchmarks achieved, ARVN ready for independent operations. The lies comfort everyone except the Vietnamese troops who'll have to live them.

Or die trying.

Chapter 50

Thunder and Steel

Dual Perspectives on Operation Linebacker
December 1972

From the Flight Log of Colonel James Webster
B-52 Squadron Commander

Another maximum effort tonight. Seventy-two B-52s hitting Hanoi's rail yards, storage areas, air defenses. Each plane carrying 108 bombs. That's 7,776 bombs in one raid. Almost believing our own propaganda—surely this will break them.

But Charlie's fighting back harder than ever. Their SAM crews are good - damn good. Three more B-52s down tonight. Crews probably dead or captured. Fourth night of heavy losses. Pentagon says the targets are worth it. Easy to say from Washington.

We bomb with computer precision, better accuracy than ever before. But at 30,000 feet, Hanoi's just a target grid. Reality is different at ground level. Remember that from my fighter days—you see the fires, the destruction, the human cost. In B-52s, we're too high to hear the screams.

Lost Johnson's crew over the rail yards. Twelve SAMs came up through the clouds like deadly fireworks. His last transmission: "Multiple launches, taking evasive..." Then silence. Another black mark on the squadron board. Another letter to write.

They say this will bring Hanoi to Paris ready to deal. After eight years of bombing, what makes these raids different? We're hitting harder, yes. But these people survived French colonialism, Japanese occupation, years of American air power. What's another few thousand tons of bombs?

From the diary of Nguyen Thi Mai
School Teacher, Hanoi

The Americans have gone mad. Night after night, their giant planes come. Not the small jets we're used to—these monsters shake the earth itself. My students no longer flinch at the explosions. They've learned to gauge which ones are dangerous, which can be ignored.

Our air defense troops fight bravely. The sky flowers with SAM explosions. Sometimes a giant B-52 falls, trailing fire. The Americans learned to jam our radar, but we learned to track them anyway. A deadly dance in the night sky.

The damage is terrible. Entire blocks vanish in single raids. But each morning, we rebuild. The Americans don't understand—they think bombing will break our will. They've forgotten that our will survived Japanese torture, French brutality, a thousand years of Chinese domination.

Little Mai asked me today why the Americans hate us so much. "They drop bombs bigger than our house," she said. How to explain that they don't hate us? They're just distant men following orders, dropping steel and fire on coordinates, not people.

Colonel Webster

Christmas Eve raid - biggest yet. Over a hundred B-52s. The
night sky over Hanoi looks like the end of the world. Anti-aircraft
fire, SAM contrails, secondaries blooming like hellish flowers. This
is what total air war looks like.

Nobody talks about the civilian casualties. We hit military targets, but with bombs this big, "military targets" becomes a flexible
term. An entire city's infrastructure is now fair game. This is what
desperation looks like—trying to win through sheer explosive ton-
nage what we couldn't win in eight years of war.

Nguyen Thi Mai

They bomb through Christmas—their own holy day. The sky
rains steel and death while their president talks of peace with hon-
or. Whose honor is served by this? Where is the honor in burning
hospitals, schools, homes?

But we endure. When the all-clear sounds, we emerge from
shelters, assess damage, begin repairs. The Americans think they're
breaking us. They're only proving what we already knew—their
power can destroy buildings but not our determination.

Colonel Webster

Final mission report: 15 B-52s lost, 93 airmen dead or captured.
Hanoi says we hit civilian targets. Probably did—bombs this big
don't care about fine distinctions. Intel says they're hurting, com-

ing to terms in Paris. But at what cost? What do you say to the wives of dead crews about "peace with honor"?

Nguyen Thi Mai

The raids finally stop. Already the rebuilding begins. The Americans never understood—you cannot bomb a people into submission who have survived centuries of invasion. Every bomb strengthened our resolve. Every crater became a symbol of resistance.

Our leaders say the Americans are ready to talk seriously in Paris now. Perhaps. But we know the truth—they're not leaving because of the damage they've done to us, but because of what the war has done to them.

Joint Entry - Same Night

The sky is silent tonight. In Hanoi, people emerge from shelters. In Guam, B-52 crews stand down. Both sides claim victory. Both sides count their dead. The ruins smolder, and peace talks resume in Paris.

Some wars end with a bang. This one ends with the realization that even the biggest bangs aren't enough.

Chapter 51

The Art of Losing Gracefully

From the Private Notes of James Peterson
State Department Note Taker
Paris Peace Conference, January 1973

Kissinger's in rare form today, playing the stern statesman for the cameras while whispering compromise to Le Duc Tho between sessions. The world sees tough negotiations. We insiders watch an elaborate dance choreographed months ago.

Everyone here knows the truth: we're not negotiating peace—we're negotiating the proper interval between American withdrawal and South Vietnam's collapse. The only real question is how to dress surrender in the clothes of peace with honor.

The South Vietnamese delegation looks shell-shocked. They know they're being abandoned, but can't say it openly. Their chief negotiator pulled me aside today, hands shaking: "You're going to let them kill us, aren't you?" What could I say? That's exactly what we're doing, just not in words anyone will print.

Today's session was pure theater. We demand guarantees for South Vietnam's independence. The North promises to respect the demilitarized zone. Everyone knows both statements are lies. The only truth here is in the silences between official pronouncements.

The real negotiations happen at late-night dinners, in hotel corridors, during smoke breaks. That's where the Americans hint at future aid to Hanoi if they'll just wait a "decent interval" before taking Saigon. Where the North Vietnamese agree to let us leave without humiliation if we'll stop propping up Thieu.

Kissinger's a master at this—making defeat sound like diplomacy. "Peace with honor," he calls it. More accurate to say "peace with face-saving lies." We're not preserving South Vietnam's independence; we're negotiating the terms of its execution.

The details are almost irrelevant: cease-fire, withdrawal timetables, prisoner exchanges. The North agrees to everything because they know none of it matters. Once we're gone, who's going to enforce these carefully worded clauses?

Most obscene are the maps—drawing cease-fire lines everyone knows won't hold, marking zones of control that will shift the moment we leave, plotting "internationally supervised" boundaries no one will respect. Hours spent arguing over lines that will be meaningless in months.

The South Vietnamese know. You see it in their eyes during the sessions. They frantically push for stronger guarantees, better terms, firmer commitments. Like a condemned man bargaining over the color of the rope.

Le Duc Tho almost seems to pity them. Today he patted their chief negotiator's shoulder during a break: "You fought well. History will remember your courage." Sounded more like a eulogy than a peace talk.

Kissinger pulled me aside after today's session. "We're not ending the war," he said. "We're ending our participation in it. There's a difference." At least he's honest in private.

The cynicism is breathtaking. We're writing a peace agreement everyone knows will be broken before the ink dries. The North will violate it immediately. We'll protest weakly. The South will scream for help. We'll express regret. And another ally will learn the cost of trusting American promises.

Tonight's draft includes beautiful language about self-determination, territorial integrity, political independence. Tomorrow we'll polish these lies until they shine. The day after, we'll sign them with great ceremony. Then we'll go home and watch South Vietnam die.

The journalists ask about "peace with honor." If they looked closer, they'd see we're negotiating our own absolution. Every clause, every paragraph aims at one goal: letting America walk away without admitting defeat.

Le Duc Tho understands perfectly. "We are giving you the chance to leave with dignity," he told Kissinger. "That is our victory."

Someone should tell the truth—that these talks aren't about peace but about creating diplomatic cover for abandonment. That we're not preserving South Vietnam's freedom but negotiating the timeline of its conquest. That this isn't diplomacy; it's a surrender masked as a settlement.

But that's not my job. I just take notes, watch the dance, record the lies. History will sort out the truth, though by then it won't matter to the people we're betraying here in Paris.

Tomorrow we'll argue more details, draw more meaningless maps, write more empty promises. The cameras will roll, the world will watch, and diplomacy will do its graceful work of dressing up reality in acceptable clothes.

Meanwhile, somewhere in South Vietnam, people who believed our promises prepare for the inevitable. Their faith in American words will cost them everything. But that won't be mentioned in the final agreement.

Peace with honor. The phrase sounds hollower every time I write it.

Chapter 52

Last Ones Out

From Letters Home by Sergeant Edward Russell
1st Battalion, 3rd Marines
February-March 1973

Dear Mom,

Strange being part of the last Marines in Vietnam. Yesterday we patrolled areas we fought for years to control. Today we're pulling out, leaving those same areas to an enemy who merely had to wait us out. Some victory.

Our ARVN counterparts watch us pack with empty eyes. They know what's coming. We've trained them, armed them, promised them everything except what they really need—the will to fight for a government that's more interested in stealing than governing.

The withdrawal has its own weird protocol. Clean the bases, burn the classified stuff, break equipment we can't take. Like moving out of an apartment, except this apartment cost 58,000 American lives.

Love,

Ed

Dear Dad,

Remember how you said wars should end with parades and clear winners? This one's ending with yard sales and equipment auctions. We're selling everything we can't ship home—trucks, generators, entire bases' worth of gear. The South Vietnamese military buys what they can. The rest goes to civilian contractors who'll probably sell it to the VC.

The helicopters run constant missions moving stuff to the ships. Same choppers that once brought us to battle now ferry filing cabinets and office furniture. The Army calls it "retrograde." We call it running away in slow motion.

Your son,

Ed

Dear Betty (sister),

You asked what it feels like. Honestly? Like being the last person at a party that ended badly. The music's stopped, the drinks are gone, and someone's going to have to clean up the mess.

The bases empty one by one. Places that once held thousands of troops now echo with the sound of scrap metal being loaded into trucks. Camp Eagle, Phu Bai, Da Nang—names that once meant something now just waiting to be renamed by the other side.

Your brother,

Ed

Dear Mom,

Had to break up a fight yesterday. One of our guys caught some ARVN troops stealing supplies. But what's stealing anymore? Everything here is already lost. We're just arguing over who gets the scraps.

The South Vietnamese officers make brave speeches about fighting on alone. Their troops look through us like we're already gone. The enemy waits patiently in the jungle. Everyone knows what's coming except the politicians in Saigon and Washington.

Love,

Ed

Dear Dad,

Last combat patrol today. Walked through villages we've "protected" for years. Kids still beg for candy, old women still bow, but there's something different in their eyes. They're already adjusting to the next chapter, the one that doesn't include us.

Funny how places remember. Every hill, every tree line, every rice paddy holds someone's war. Now they'll hold someone else's peace. Or someone else's war. Not our problem anymore, they tell us.

Your son,

Ed

Dear Betty,

The giant map in our TOC shows the evacuation schedule. Every day more red areas turn green—"processed for withdrawal." Like a tide going out, leaving who knows what on the beach.

We're not supposed to talk about abandonment. The official line is "Vietnamization successfully completed." But you can't spin this much sadness. We're leaving people behind who believed our promises. No way to make that look good.

Ed

Dear Mom,

Final days now. The VC don't even hide anymore. They watch us leave, counting down with us. Their propaganda banners say "Same old story—French left, Americans leaving, Vietnamese staying."

Hard to argue with that.

Love,

Ed

Dear Dad,

You asked if we accomplished anything. The official answer is we held the line against communism, bought time for South Vietnam to stand on its own. The real answer? We killed and died here for eight years just to leave it the way we found it. Maybe worse.

The last patrol comes in. The last perimeter is drawn. The last watch is posted. Tomorrow we load the ships. The war that defined our generation ends not with a bang but with a company inventory.

Your son,

Ed

Dear All,

On the ship now, watching the coast fade. Nine years, 58,000 dead Americans, who knows how many Vietnamese, all those billions of dollars, all that hope and pain and sacrifice—vanishing like smoke.

Someone just said, "Last one out, turn off the lights." But we're leaving the lights on. Also the ammunition, the bases, the equipment, and a lot of promises. History will sort out who lost Vietnam. Right now, it just feels like we all did.

They're playing "We Gotta Get Out of This Place" on someone's radio. The Navy calls this "offshore withdrawal." The VC are calling it victory. The South Vietnamese are calling it betrayal.

Me? I'm just calling it over.
Coming home soon.

Love,

Ed

Chapter 53

Watching It Fall

From the War Diary of Colonel Tran Van Minh
South Vietnamese 18th Infantry Division
June 1973 - December 1974

June 1973

Another ammunition request denied. "Budget constraints," they say. Yesterday we faced a VC attack with artillery pieces but no shells. Three years ago, American jets would have been overhead within minutes. Now we pray for helicopter support that never comes.

My men desert in growing numbers. Can't blame them. Their pay doesn't cover food for their families—when it comes at all. The Americans left us their bases, their equipment, their war. But not the means to sustain any of it.

August 1973

Congress cuts aid again. Saigon responds by closing another twenty outposts. Each abandoned position becomes an enemy base. My old friend Colonel Hien says it's like watching gangrene spread up a limb. We keep retreating, keep concentrating our forces, keep giving up territory we spent years defending.

The enemy grows bolder. They know we can't replace losses—in men or material. Each broken tank, each crashed helicopter, each expended shell brings us closer to the end. Their supply lines from the North run freely now. No American planes to threaten them.

October 1973

Fuel shortages ground most of our air force. Had to abandon three hills today—couldn't get air support, couldn't resupply the troops. The Americans taught us to fight their way—with massive firepower, with mobility, with air supremacy. Now we have none of these things.

A captain asked me today: "Sir, what are we fighting for?" Once I had answers. Now I watch Saigon's generals build villas while our soldiers go hungry. Watch politicians steal aid money while our wounded lack medicine. What am I supposed to tell him?

January 1974

My unit now defends twice the territory with half the men we had last year. The enemy probes, tests, finds our weak spots. They know time is on their side. Their Russian tanks and Chinese

weapons flow south unimpeded while we cannibalize parts to keep
one helicopter flying.

Tried to explain our situation to the American attaché. He took
notes, promised to "raise concerns through appropriate channels."
His eyes said what his mouth couldn't: You're on your own now.

April 1974

Lost another district today. No fighting—the local forces simply
switched sides. Their commander made a deal: keep his position,
keep his men alive, just change uniforms. More and more I hear of
such arrangements. The rats know which ship is sinking.

Visited the American base at Bien Hoa—now our base. Empty
hangars, abandoned barracks, rusting equipment. Like a museum
of lost power. Some buildings still have old U.S. unit signs, fading
in the sun. Even the weeds growing through the concrete seem
American somehow.

July 1974

Our intelligence reports North Vietnamese divisions moving
south openly now. Tanks, artillery, truck convoys—all down the
Ho Chi Minh Trail in broad daylight. Three years ago, American
bombers would have destroyed them. Now we watch helplessly as
the forces gathering to destroy us grow stronger.

Had to execute a deserter today. He was selling ammunition
to the VC—said he needed money to feed his children. His last
words: "I die for nothing, like our country." The firing squad wept.

September 1974

Saigon lives in fantasy. The president talks of victory while his wife buys real estate in France. Generals issue brave statements from air-conditioned offices while their families quietly disappear to America or Paris. Everyone can see what's coming except those paid not to see it.

My own family begs me to make plans. "You fought bravely," my wife says. "Now fight for your children's future." But how can I leave while my men still hold the line? What kind of officer abandons his troops to their fate?

November 1974

The North Vietnamese don't even bother with guerrilla tactics anymore. They mass conventional forces, knowing we lack the fuel and ammunition to respond. Each week brings news of another unit surrendering, another province falling, another defensive line crumbling.

We who fought with Americans, learned their tactics, believed their promises, now face the consequences of their departure. They called it "peace with honor." We call it abandonment. They moved on to other concerns while we await the executioner.

December 1974

Christmas brings news of another aid cut. Congress tires of supporting what they call a "corrupt, failed state." They forget this is the state they created, corrupted by their money, failed by their departure.

The end is coming. Everyone feels it. The enemy advances, our forces retreat, the clock ticks down. Soon the world will watch South Vietnam die and cluck about the "tragedy." But the real tragedy isn't that we're losing. It's that we were never given a real chance to win.

Tonight I burn my diary. Tomorrow I tell my men what I can no longer deny—we are already defeated. The only question is how many more must die before Saigon admits it.

The Americans taught us everything about war except how to survive their departure.

Chapter 54

The Last Campaign

Private Nguyen Van Tuan
North Vietnamese Army, 2nd Corps
March-April 1975

For six years, I walked through jungles carrying an AK-47. Now I ride in an American tank, one our enemies abandoned intact, still half-full of fuel. The gun sights are in English. The radio crackles with frantic ARVN transmissions. Even their panic sounds American somehow.

Yesterday we passed through a village I used to raid as a guerrilla. Then, we came at night, quick and silent. Now our column stretches for miles—tanks, trucks, artillery, all captured, all heading south. Old women who once fed us in secret now throw flowers openly. Children wave flags. But some faces show fear. They wonder if we come as liberators or conquerors.

Near Pleiku, we overran an ARVN position. Their officers had fled, leaving teenage soldiers to face us alone. When we approached, they threw down their rifles—American M-16s, still gleaming with oil. One boy started crying. "We're all Vietnamese," he said. "Why are we killing each other?" I had no answer.

The Americans taught them to depend on air power, on helicopters, on big guns. Now their skies are empty. Their artillery has no shells. Their radios call for help that will never come. We advance so fast our maps can't keep up. Each morning we wake in a different war.

Outside Ban Me Thuot, I saw something that haunts me. An ARVN captain stood by the road, saluting as his men fled past. Just standing there, ramrod straight, tears running down his face. Our tank commander ordered us not to shoot. Some dignity should be respected, even in defeat.

My father fought the French at Dien Bien Phu. "War is not about weapons," he told me. "It's about will." Now I understand. Our enemies have American tanks, American planes, American training. But their will belongs to a nation that no longer exists. We fight for unification. What do they fight for?

The roads south are strange rivers—half military retreat, half civilian exodus. Abandoned tanks block refugee carts. Soldiers throw away their uniforms, try to disappear into the crowd. We let many go. They are our countrymen, however misguided. Tomorrow we must all be Vietnamese together.

Near Xuan Loc, real resistance at last. For three days we fought soldiers who remembered their pride. Our artillery crushed them anyway. Walking through the wreckage, I found a family photo in a bunker—mother, father, children, everyone smiling. I buried it. Some memories shouldn't be captured.

In a village market, an old man who sold us rice wine said something striking: "First the French came and called it peace. Then the Americans came and called it democracy. Now you come calling it liberation. But we are still here, still Vietnamese, still eating rice from the same fields."

The end comes faster than anyone expected. Like a dam breaking, like a fever breaking, like a heart breaking. Twenty years of division dissolve in weeks. We ride captured tanks down American-built roads, chasing a retreating army that melts away before u s.

Last night I dreamed of the jungle wars—the hiding, the ambushes, the terror of helicopter gunships. Now we advance in daylight, proud flags flying. But somehow the old way felt cleaner. We knew who we were then—barefoot soldiers fighting the world's greatest power. Who are we now, driving American tanks to kill other Vietnamese?

Outside Saigon, the roads fill with people fleeing the "liberators." They fear revenge, reprisals, re-education. We're told to tell them: "Vietnamese don't kill Vietnamese anymore. The war is over." But two decades of lies don't die easily. Trust takes longer to build than tanks take to drive south.

Tomorrow we enter Saigon. Already we can see the city's glow against the night sky. American helicopters swarm like desperate dragonflies, lifting the last believers in their lost cause to safety. Let them go. Our victory is not over America—they left two years ago. Our victory is over the myth that Vietnam could ever be permanently divided.

But tonight, watching those helicopters, I wonder: What do we really win? A destroyed country. A traumatized people. A generation raised on war, now asked to live in peace. Cities full of Americans' abandoned children. Streets full of their abandoned dreams.

Vietnam will be one nation tomorrow. But at what cost? And what do we do with unity once we have it?

The tank's engine rumbles. Saigon waits. History beckons. But the taste of victory is mixed with tears.

Chapter 55

The Last Days of Saigon

April 1975

Frank Matthews
Political Officer, U.S. Embassy
April 15, 1975

The cables from Washington grow more frantic. "Prepare for evacuation" but "avoid panic." "Process key Vietnamese personnel" but "maintain normal operations." "Be ready for anything" but "don't show obvious signs of preparation." They want us to organize the end of a country without admitting it's ending.

Today I shredded my contact lists. Names of Vietnamese who helped us, worked with us, believed in us. Ten years of relationships reduced to confetti. Through my office window, I watch the endless stream of people outside the embassy gates, waving papers, pleading for visas. We've started calling it "the wailing wall."

Ambassador Martin still insists we're not evacuating. "Orderly departure," he calls it. But the CIA station is burning files 24/7. The Marine guards practice helicopter evacuation drills on the roof. Even the embassy cats know something's wrong—they've stopped lounging in the courtyard.

Tran Van Minh
Former Deputy Minister, South Vietnamese Government
April 20, 1975

My American friends aren't answering their phones. Their houses are empty, their offices closed. Even their servants have disappeared. The rats always know when to leave the ship.

My wife begs me to use my connections, get us out before it's too late. But how can I abandon the country I helped build? Even if it was built on American promises that turned to dust.

The money changers offer a million piasters for one U.S. dollar. Last year it was 750 piasters. Last week it was 100,000. The black market speaks truth when politicians lie.

Sarah Collins
CIA Communications Officer
April 22, 1975

Another eighteen-hour day destroying files. My hands are black with shredder dust. The incinerator runs so hot it's melting the bricks. Still, we can't keep up. Thirty years of intelligence operations—informant lists, operation reports, agent evaluations—all has to go.

The worst are the agent files. Each one represents someone who trusted us, worked for us, risks death if captured. We're supposed to evacuate them. But there are thousands, and our helicopters can carry dozens. The math is brutal.

Station Chief told us to prioritize: "First destroy anything that could identify Vietnamese who worked with us. Then networks and methods. Last, general intelligence." He didn't say what we all know—we're choosing who lives and who dies with every file we burn.

Lieutenant David Anderson
Marine Security Guard
April 24, 1975

The crush at the gates gets worse every day. People wave documents, photos with American soldiers, anything to prove they're connected to us. Some throw their babies over the wall, hoping we'll at least save their children.

Ambassador keeps telling us to maintain normal security procedures. What's normal about watching former ministers sleep in their cars outside the embassy? What's normal about Vietnamese colonels begging Marines for help? What's normal about planning your own surrender?

We're down to two responses: "Get on the list" or "Sorry, can't help." The list is already too long. The "sorry" breaks your heart every time.

Nguyen Thi Mai
Secretary, U.S. Aid Mission
April 26, 1975

My American boss left last week. "Processing paperwork," he said. "Back in a few days." His desk is still covered with unfinished reports. The office plants need water. He's not coming back.

The embassy promised visas for all Vietnamese employees. Now they say only those with ten years' service. Tomorrow maybe fifteen. The day after, who knows? Every hour the rules change. Every hour the North Vietnamese get closer.

My sister says I'm crazy to stay at work. "They'll punish anyone who helped the Americans," she warns. But where else can I go? At least here I have a chance. Outside, there are only rumors and fear.

Captain Mike Wilson
Air America Pilot
April 28, 1975

Flew six missions today. Not supposed to call them evacuations—"personnel transport" is the official term. Tell that to the people fighting to get on my chopper, or the ones we have to push away.

The city's gone crazy. People selling everything they own for a chance at escape. Downtown, the streets are full of abandoned cars. Rich people's villas are empty, their swimming pools turned green. But the bars are full—everyone drinking like it's their last chance. Maybe it is.

Had to dust off from a pickup point when the crowd rushed the chopper. They'd have torn it apart trying to get aboard. Through my windscreen, I watched a man in a business suit kneeling, holding up his children. Hardest thing I've ever done, lifting off without them.

Colonel Bao Van Nguyen
North Vietnamese Army, 203rd Tank Regiment
April 29, 1975

Our tanks wait in the tree lines north of Saigon. Through binoculars, I watch American helicopters swarming around their embassy like angry bees. Their evacuation is already a rout, though they'll never call it that.

Twenty years we fought them. Now they run, leaving their allies, their equipment, their promises. Some of my men want immediate revenge. I tell them: "Let them go. Our victory is complete enough without more blood."

The radio brings reports of South Vietnamese units surrendering en masse. Their American advisors gone, their president fled, their generals escaping with gold-filled suitcases. Tomorrow we enter Saigon. Today we watch an empire abandon its friends.

James Monroe
Consular Officer, U.S. Embassy
April 30, 1975

Dawn breaks over chaos. The embassy courtyard is a maze of desperate people. Vietnamese who worked for us for decades. Wives and children of officials. Anyone with a claim, a connection, a hope.

The choppers can't keep up. Every landing space is full—the embassy roof, the parking lot, neighboring buildings. We form human chains, pass people up like sandbags in a flood. No more paperwork, no more procedures. Just grab who you can and go.

Ambassador Martin still at his desk, signing papers like it's a normal day. Outside his window, Marines tear up classified documents, scatter them in the swimming pool. The embassy gates are locked but crowds try to climb the walls. Gunshots in the distance getting closer.

Final cable from State Department: "Evacuate all remaining Americans. Ambassador has authority to permit evacuation of high-risk Vietnamese, depending on available space. Exercise discretion. Good luck."

Discretion. They mean choose who lives and who dies. Choose who we save and who we leave to face the consequences of believing in us.

Time's up. The last choppers wait. History will judge us for this day, but right now there's only the sound of rotor blades and the sight of a city dying.

Somewhere a clerk will write that Saigon fell on April 30, 1975. But those of us who were there know it died by inches over many days, each hour marked by another broken promise, another abandoned ally, another American door closing on Vietnamese hands.

Let the historians debate who lost Vietnam. Those of us who lived its last days know: we all did.

Chapter 56

The Fall

April 30, 1975
0530 Hours
Sergeant James Connor
Marine Security Guard, U.S. Embassy

Lady Ace 09 lifts off with Ambassador Martin. He carried the embassy flag under his arm, refused to look back. Below us, the courtyard's still full of Vietnamese. We can't take them all. Someone's got to be last, got to close the door, got to end this.

The orders come clear: "Tiger, Tiger, Tiger." Initiate final evacuation. Get all remaining Americans out. Break down the doors to the roof. Destroy the radio equipment. Burn the last files.

Through my helmet radio: "Lady Ace reports ground fire from Saigon streets. Negative on return. All remaining lifts by Air America from embassy roof only."

The faces below us understand. They know we're leaving them behind.

0645 Hours
Tran Van Hieu
Presidential Palace Guard

President Minh orders us to lay down arms. "Further resistance futile," he says. "Avoid bloodshed." Twenty years of war ends with words of surrender spoken into a radio microphone.

Outside, the streets fill with surrendering soldiers. They strip off their uniforms, leave their weapons in neat piles. Some cry. Some burn their papers. Some just sit and stare at nothing.

The palace feels empty already, though we still guard its gates. What are we guarding it from? For whom?

0800 Hours
Colonel Bui Tin
North Vietnamese Army

Our tanks move through Saigon's streets uncontested. White flags hang from windows. Discarded South Vietnamese uniforms litter the gutters. The city surrenders not with a bang but with exhausted silence.

At a street corner, an old woman offers our troops tea. "Welcome, liberators," she says. But her eyes say something else. Everyone here has survival in their eyes.

Radio from command: "Proceed to Presidential Palace. Accept surrender. Maintain order. Prevent reprisals."

0900 Hours
Sarah Collins
CIA Communications Officer

Last Flight Out

The embassy roof's a madhouse. Too many people, too few choppers. Marines form chains, pulling up the lucky ones, pushing back the rest. Below, people still scale the walls despite the tear gas.

Final radio check. All stations gone dark. Destroy the last crypto gear. Someone's crying in the comm room. Twenty-five years of American presence in Vietnam ends with a sledgehammer to a radio set.

The chopper lifts off. Below us, the embassy gates finally break. The crowd pours in, but it's too late. We're gone. God forgive us.

1000 Hours
Captain Nguyen Van Thieu
South Vietnamese Air Force
(Last Flight from Tan Son Nhut)

My Huey's overloaded but they keep coming. Families with children, soldiers, civilians—all trying to escape. We can barely clear the runway. Below us, Saigon burns.

Looking back, I see North Vietnamese tanks entering the air-base. The runways where American B-52s once ruled now belong to Russian-built armor. The wheel turns.

Fuel gauge shows empty. We'll never make it to the ships. Maybe the ocean's a better fate than what we leave behind.

1100 Hours
Le Duan
Political Officer, North Vietnamese Army

Our tanks reach the Presidential Palace. The gates open without resistance. Inside, President Minh waits with his cabinet. "I have been waiting since morning to transfer power to you," he says.

Our colonel replies: "You cannot give up what you do not have." History speaks through his words. This was never their country to surrender.

Outside, our soldiers raise the liberation flag. Twenty years of war end with a piece of cloth rising in the humid air.

1300 Hours
Peter Chang
Reuters Correspondent
Last Western Journalist in Saigon

The city transforms before my eyes. Viet Cong flags appear from nowhere. People who yesterday praised America now praise Uncle Ho. Everyone here knows how to survive occupation—they've had centuries of practice.

In the market, traders already price goods in North Vietnamese dong. A barber takes down his sign advertising "American-style haircuts." History moves fast when it finally moves.

The telex machine still works. My last dispatch: "Saigon has fallen. Stop. South Vietnam ceases to exist. Stop. A nation dies not with a bang but with helicopters running away. Stop."

1500 Hours
Sister Marie Claire
Carmelite Convent, Saigon

The guns are silent for the first time in memory. Our chapel fills with people seeking sanctuary, though from what? The war is over. The killing should be over. But fear has its own momentum.

From our bell tower, I watch North Vietnamese soldiers direct traffic, maintain order. They seem surprised by their own victory. Yesterday's enemies now control the streets where they once hid.

The evening bells ring as always. God's time pays no attention to man's wars.

1700 Hours
Major Nguyen Van Minh
North Vietnamese 203rd Tank Regiment

Victory feels strange. No resistance, no last stand, just empty streets and surrendering soldiers. We expected a fortress; we found a hollow shell.

My men raise the flag over the U.S. Embassy. Inside, abandoned papers drift like leaves. The Americans left their allies but took their furniture. Even their defeat shows their priorities.

Radio from Hanoi: "Saigon is now Ho Chi Minh City." But names change easier than hearts. The real battle—reunifying our divided people—begins now.

2000 Hours
Anonymous Diary Entry
Found in Abandoned Saigon Apartment

The city changes its face like a chameleon. People who yesterday spoke of democracy now quote Ho Chi Minh. Those who could not escape now learn to adapt.

Tonight the curfew empties the streets. Dogs bark at unfamiliar patrols. Somewhere, someone burns photographs, documents,
memories. The past goes up in smoke.

The war ends not with yesterday's bang but with today's whim-
per. We who remain learn the first lesson of survival: how to forget
who we were by remembering who we must become.

Midnight
Radio Broadcast
Voice of Vietnam

"Attention citizens: The liberation of Saigon is complete. The
puppet regime has surrendered. The American imperialists have
fled. The revolution triumphs. Vietnam is one again."

In the dark, the city holds its breath. One war ends. Another—the war of reconciliation—begins. The victors and the vanquished must now learn to live as one people.

The clock strikes twelve. April 30, 1975, becomes May 1. Yesterday's Saigon becomes tomorrow's Ho Chi Minh City. The future
arrives on tank tracks, carrying both hope and fear in its iron heart.

Chapter 57

The Master's Final Observation

The Thoughts of Confucius Upon Viewing Vietnam
Year of the Rabbit (Late 1975)

I, who taught of harmony between Heaven and Earth, return one final time to this troubled land. The war that tore Vietnam apart has ended, yet peace brings its own kind of violence. The victors speak of unity while building re-education camps. The vanquished learn to swallow bitterness with their morning rice.

In Ho Chi Minh City—the place that was Saigon—I watch the transformation. Revolutionary slogans replace advertising billboards. People who once quoted Jefferson now quote Marx. The chameleon survives by changing colors, and the Vietnamese are history's greatest survivors.

At the docks where American ships once unloaded abundance, Russian freighters now bring austerity. The new rulers wear simple clothes and speak of equality, but power remains power, whether wrapped in democratic words or revolutionary rhetoric. Did I not teach that the name should match the reality? They call it liberation, but I see new chains replacing old ones.

Most striking is how the Vietnamese absorb this latest conqueror, as they absorbed all previous ones. In temples, old women burn incense before ancestral tablets while mouthing revolutionary phrases. Children learn communist doctrine in schools, then come home to families still structured on Confucian principles. The surface changes; the depths remain.

Walking through a New Economic Zone, I observe former Saigon businessmen learning to farm with borrowed tools. The revolution promises to remake society, yet follows patterns old as civilization—the victors redistribute land, exile the educated, remake the social order. When I spoke of moral reformation, did I imagine it would come at gunpoint?

Yet there is hope in the persistence of ancient ways. In village temples, I see offerings to both revolutionary martyrs and traditional spirits. Farmers whisper "Comrade" in public but teach their children to bow before family altars in private. The revolution can change many things, but cannot change the Vietnamese soul.

The war's wounds run deep. Brothers who fought on opposite sides now live in uneasy peace. Winners and losers share the same streets, shop in the same markets, but carry different memories. I watch children playing in swimming pools of abandoned villas while their parents adjust to new realities. The young adapt quickly; the old learn to forget selectively.

Most painful is the exile of so many. Boat people risk death on hostile seas, seeking freedom at any cost. Those who helped the Americans hide their past or face punishment. The lucky ones fled with the last helicopters. The others learn to edit their biographies, erasing dangerous associations like calligraphers removing unwanted characters.

In Hanoi, the victors build their new society with old bricks. They speak of revolution but understand tradition's power. Their cadres study Soviet economics while consulting fortune tellers.

Even Marx must bow to ancestral spirits here. Did I not teach that change, to be lasting, must respect what came before?

The Americans have gone, leaving behind abandoned bases, mixed-race children, and memories that fade like old photographs. Already they become legend—their PX stores, their dollars, their naive belief that salvation could come through helicopters and aid programs. Vietnam swallowed their pride as it swallowed all previous pride, turning martial defeat into spiritual victory.

Looking to the future, I see hard times ahead. The revolution's promises will meet reality's constraints. Rice does not grow better for being planted by communist hands. The gods do not grant special favor to those who quote correct doctrine. Vietnam must find its own way between the extremes that tore it apart.

Yet I also see strength in this wounded nation. The Vietnamese endure, as they have always endured. They take what is useful from each invader—French administration, American technology, Soviet ideology—and make it their own. They bend like bamboo in the storm, but their roots run deep in ancient soil.

Let those who read these final observations understand: Vietnam's tragedy was not that it failed to embrace the new, but that the new came with such violence. Not that it resisted change, but that change arrived wearing foreign faces. Not that it disappointed its would-be saviors, but that it refused to be saved on others' terms.

The wheel turns. Today's victors will face tomorrow's challenges. Today's truth will become tomorrow's lie. But through it all, Vietnam remains Vietnam. The rice grows, the ancestors watch, the people endure. They have outlasted Chinese emperors, French colonials, Japanese conquerors, and American liberators. They will outlast this revolution too.

Perhaps that is the final lesson of this long war: Vietnam cannot be remade by foreign hands, whether holding dollars or rifles. It changes in its own way, at its own pace, following patterns laid down in centuries of survival. The surface may wear strange colors, but the heart beats to rhythms old as humanity.

I go now from this troubled land, leaving it to find its own harmony between past and future, between North and South, between the eternal Vietnam and the new world rushing at it like a storm wind. May Heaven grant it the wisdom to preserve what is precious while discarding what must be discarded.

The rest is silence, and the sound of rain falling on rice fields that have outlived all theories of how they should be tended.

Also by Barry Robbins

Voices of the Civil War
Voices of the American Revolution
Tears of the Titans
American Wake-Up Call
Three Questions in the Ethereal
The Ethereal Concerto

About the author

Barry hails from Philadelphia and built a career with a prominent international accounting firm, taking him to New
York, Washington, D.C., and San Francisco before a new chapter
brought him to Finland. He and his Finnish wife adopted two
daughters from China, and their family lived in Helsinki for twelve
years before he returned to the U.S., now calling Florida home. His
years in Finland gave him a new lens through which to view life in
America.

Barry's literary work blends satire, history, and whimsy. Known
for his Trump satires, including "The Weave", he's earned three
gold medals for his sharp wit. His curiosity also led to the Ethereal
Bar, a magical place where legends of history stop by for poignant
interviews.

Barry's most recent works reveal a thoughtful turn: "Tears of the
Titans" examines the regrets of historical icons, while "Voices of the
Civil War", "Voices of the American Revolution", and "Voices of
Vietnam" bring an immersive, personal lens to these tumultuous
periods. With a knack for balancing wit and insight, Barry's writing invites readers to explore history from new, intimate perspectives.

www.ingramcontent.com/pod-product-compliance
Ingram Content Group UK Ltd.
Pitfield, Milton Keynes, MK11 3LW, UK
UKHW022353030225
454636UK00008B/103